Dear Reader,

Did you ever notice that [a man who] makes those around him [believe] that no power on earth can stop ~~him~~ from getting what he wants?

An illusion, of course, and one that makes the woman who's falling in love with him wonder what lies behind that tough facade. She'll look for his vulnerabilities— surely he has some! She'll arm herself with each one, *use* them if she must. And all the while, she'll hope to find a particular weakness, one that makes him vulnerable only to her.

Because sometimes in a moment of need, a man's greatest weakness can turn out to be his greatest strength.

I hope you'll enjoy Elissa's quest as she probes beneath the tough exterior of Captain Jesse Garrett...to find the surprise awaiting her there...

Happy Reading!

Donna Sterling

# How could anyone lie so convincingly?

Jesse almost had Elissa believing he had come straight from some gruelling mission that he wasn't yet ready to discuss. 'Call me Jesse.' It was an order, not a request. At her startled glance, he uttered, 'I've waited a long time to hear you say it, Elissa.'

The subdued passion behind the words rattled her. Inexplicably, she felt like crying. She drew in a breath, fortifying herself against the drugging effect of his nearness and the unmistakable message in his bold, heated stare. He wanted her. And though he hadn't made a move to touch her, she felt his touch and thrilled to it.

When she finally found her voice, it shook. 'Did you bring the waiver of parental status that I sent you?'

Although his expression hadn't changed, he suddenly looked dangerous. Intimidating. Every inch the battle-hardened commando. 'No, I did not. What makes you think I'd ever give up my son?'

\* \* \*

'**Donna Sterling** is clearly a top talent. With this brilliantly scribed tale she demonstrates the genius that makes her a rising star.'
*—Affaire de Coeur*

# POSSESSING ELISSA

BY

DONNA STERLING

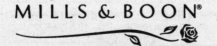

MILLS & BOON®

*MILLS & BOON and MILLS & BOON with the Rose Device
are registered trademarks of the publisher.
TEMPTATION is a registered trademark of
Harlequin Enterprises Limited, used under licence.*

*First published in Great Britain 1997
by Harlequin Mills & Boon Limited,
Eton House, 18-24 Paradise Road, Richmond, Surrey TW9 1SR*

© Donna Fejes 1997

ACKNOWLEDGEMENT
My heartfelt thanks...
To Kosmar, whose music inspired the creation of Jesse, To my
critique group—Melissa Beck, Marge Gargosh, Susan Goggins and
Carina Rock—for their advice and support, To my family, for the
love that sustains me, and to Susan Sheppard, whose open mind and
warm enthusiasm set my soul free. This book wouldn't have
happened without you.

ISBN 0 263 80654 5
*21-9711*
*Printed and bound in Great Britain
by Caledonian International Book Manufacturing Ltd, Glasgow*

# 1

*THE DAMNED CONDOM had busted.* That bothersome little detail flashed with neon clarity through Jesse's
memory as he reread the letter for the umpteenth time
in two days.

> Dear Captain Garrett,
>   Hope this letter finds you safe and well. You
> might not like the news I have to share. I'm preg-
> nant, and the baby is unquestionably yours. Don't
> worry—I won't complicate your life. I'm perfectly
> able to raise this child on my own. He's due in July.
> Let me know your thoughts.
>
>                                   Sincerely,
>                                   Elissa Sinclair

Belted into the seat of the homeward-bound army
transport as it lifted off from the small airstrip, Jesse
Garrett stared at the linen stationery until the handwrit-
ing blurred before his eyes. In the two days since he'd
collected his back mail, the shock of this letter's news
had somewhat worn off. He was able now to concentrate on the woman who had written the brief, impersonal note.

She hadn't been brief or impersonal the night they'd
met. And she hadn't called him "Captain Garrett."

Of all the details he'd forgotten about her, Jesse re-

membered the heat that had gunned through his veins
when she'd whispered his name. And he remembered
her mouth. Smooth, sweet and incredibly arousing.
And the provocative feel of her in his arms, writhing beneath him in bed... These were his memories of Elissa
Sinclair; dreamlike impressions that had stayed with
him, warming him, stirring him, night after night
throughout the entire hellish year.

*Get real, Garrett.* She couldn't possibly have been as
good as all that. It had been his last night of leave, and if
his gut instinct about this covert mission had proved
correct, it would have been his last night on this earth
with a woman. Imminent death, mused Jesse, has a
surefire way of intensifying one's appreciation of pleasure.

Striving to remember more about her, Jesse retrieved
a second letter from his coat pocket—the last letter she
had sent him, dated months after the first.

Dear Captain Garrett,
   Enclosed is a birth certificate for Cody Sinclair,
born on July 8. Please note your name appears as
"father." If you care to claim paternal responsibility, advise me immediately. If not, complete and
notarize the enclosed legal document.
   Once your waiver has been received, you will
never again be connected with this matter. Contact
me at the above address.
                                    Elissa Sinclair

Jesse shoved both letters into the inner pocket of his
military overcoat. He supposed if he had answered the
first letter, the second might have been friendlier. But

he hadn't read either until two days ago. And it was already October.

Which made his son three months old.

*His son.* Jesse had little doubt that the baby was his. Why would Elissa lie? She was asking absolutely nothing from him; in fact, she seemed anxious to cut him out of the picture altogether. The timing was precisely right, the condom had broken, and his cousin Dean had raised hell all the way to the airport the next morning for "playing fast and loose with a woman like Elissa," one of Dean's closest friends since his freshman year in college. "Damn you, Jesse, she's not the kind of woman you're used to."

He'd been right about that. Jesse had known she was different within moments of meeting her. Classier. Softer. Infinitely beyond his reach. And he had wanted her more than anything he'd ever wanted in his life.

Guilt rumbled through him. Had he deliberately seduced her? He didn't remember it that way, but now he wasn't sure. How had the pregnancy affected her life? She was some kind of schoolteacher, wasn't she? In a small southern town. Jesse winced. Single and pregnant couldn't have been easy. Was she resentful? Would she take it out on the child?

At the thought, an unfamiliar pang clutched at Jesse. *Would the boy be loved?*

Cody. His name was Cody.

Jesse tightened his fists as an odd protectiveness washed through him. Elissa obviously expected him to sign a few forms, then be on his way. Before he'd left the base today, he had signed a few forms, all right. But not the ones she'd sent him. He had wanted to start the legal ball rolling so there'd be no doubt about his intentions.

Staring through the thick, smudged window, Jesse watched as the hazy green expanse of forest below gave way to the gray shadows of mountains. The men around him talked, laughed and lied about what awaited them stateside.

A sudden vibration shuddered through the aircraft. Jesse, like the others, ignored it. The vibration worsened; the engine spluttered. Conversations died. Jesse cursed with impatience. Not another delay. With his luck, they'd have to land in the middle of godforsaken nowhere.

It wasn't until the pilot's panicked voice crackled over the intercom that Jesse's premonition of death returned, no longer just the vague intuition riding heavy in his gut, but a looming, rational possibility.

*Not now.* His silent pronouncement was a fierce resolution, uncompromising and absolute. *I won't die now.*

The engine cut off; the pilot cursed. The nose angled down into a dive. Panic broke out among the men. Jesse refused to give in to it. He had to get back to Georgia to meet his son. To make sure he had a better start in life than he himself had had. To change his name to Cody Garrett.

And to douse with cold reality the memories of Elissa that made him want so damned badly to get back to her. He wouldn't rest until he had done at least that much.

Nothing, but nothing, would stop him.

TIPTOEING IN HER fuzzy purple slipper-socks past the sleeping children, Elissa gently laid the newborn down into the crib and covered her with a silky baby blanket.

Barely daring to breathe, Elissa then glanced into the corner crib where her own son dozed, his diapered rump high in the air, his chubby legs tucked beneath him. She removed the pacifier from his bow-shaped little mouth, brushed a kiss against his milk-scented cheek and tiptoed out of the room.

Nap time. At last, an hour or two of peace.

If she worked quickly, she could have her kitchen cleaned before the kids woke up. Savoring the time she'd have to herself, she clicked on her radio, turned the volume down low and found a station playing soft jazz blues. She bent over a bouquet of roses from Dean, indulged in a whiff of their fragrance, then set about her cleaning chores.

It had been one hectic morning, she reflected, moving her hips to the beat as she mopped up soup. Nine-month-old Jennifer, in a teething frenzy, had gnawed on everything...including Joshua's finger, which he'd obligingly stuck in her mouth. Cody had been whiny except while in his swing, which required cranking every five minutes. Heather, recently introduced to the potty concept, spent the morning racing to her potty-chair, whether she needed to or not.

Five children, mused Elissa as she tossed baby-food jars into her recycling bin, were harder to handle than she'd expected. Then again, she *was* managing to keep them all safe, dry, well fed and reasonably happy.

And she did so need the money.

She applied her soapy dishrag to the cookie mush and thought back to her days of lucrative paychecks, panty hose, lacquered nails and reasonable schedules. She couldn't help a certain wistfulness. Seven years of college, five years of professional experience, and where was she now? Chiseling a dried Noodle-O off a high-chair leg.

Every career had its challenges.

Resolutely she concentrated on the bright side. Her life plan had changed—drastically, yes, but not necessarily for the worse. She couldn't imagine living now without Cody. He was her joy, her sunshine, her happiness.

The ringing of the telephone startled her. She dropped her dishrag into the sink, dried her hands on the apron that covered her faded jeans and hurried to the phone.

"Elissa, is this a good time to talk?"

She sank down onto a kitchen chair and blew her dark, wayward bangs off her forehead, happy to hear another adult voice. "It's fine, Mom. They're all out for the count."

"So, have you made up your mind about Dean yet?"

Elissa squeezed her eyes shut. She'd known this was coming. "No, I told you I wanted to think about it. Marriage is a big step."

"But you've known him since your freshman year in college, Elissa, and he's been so good to you through this entire ordeal." *Better than you deserve.* Her mother hadn't actually said it, but Elissa heard the implication.

"Yes, Dean's a good friend, but we've never actually been more than that. I think he sees himself as my knight in shining armor. It's sweet of him, but I'm not sure if I—"

"Elissa, honey, your son's already three months old, and you're still single. How do you think he'll feel when he's old enough to understand his...you know... status?"

She stiffened, her hackles raised. "What exactly do you mean by status?" Politically incorrect words like *illegitimate*—and worse—hovered somewhere on the line between them, mercifully unspoken, but nonetheless hurtful.

"Oh, Elissa, you know as well as I do that a husband like Dean would mean security for you and Cody. Why, health care alone costs a fortune these days. Believe me, honey, you could use a knight in shining armor right now."

"I wouldn't marry anyone just for financial security." But she had to admit to herself that the small profit she made from her home day-care business was barely enough for rent, food and diapers. A hard-working, responsible partner *would* make their lives much easier.

"If you won't do it for financial reasons, then what about social? Once you're married, even *this* community will forgive and forget your...er..."

"Fall from grace?"

"I wasn't going to say that. But you know what I mean. Why, I'll even bet the school would rehire you."

"I wouldn't go back, Mom, even if they asked." The ludicrous relief on the faces of the administrators when she'd handed in her resignation had been almost laughable—if it hadn't cut so deeply. She hadn't been fired for her pregnancy; *that* was forbidden by law. But the disapproval of her co-workers—and the fact that the community would have questioned her influence over its impressionable teens—was enough for her to withdraw from her hard-earned position. Why submit herself or her child to public censure?

And then there was the real reason she'd quit her career as a high school counselor. She didn't deserve it. The position required impeccable judgment and clear-cut vision. She simply didn't qualify anymore.

"Elissa, you could hardly blame the school or the

community for disapproving of an unmarried high
school counselor who gets herself knocked up."

"Mother!"

"And in this town, everyone knows you weren't even
dating anyone seriously. How could they trust you to
properly guide troubled teens if you yourself—"

"I know, Mom, I know. Let's just brand a scarlet *A* on
my forehead and talk about something else, shall we?"

"Honey, you're a mother now, and it's time for you to
wake up and smell the orange blossoms. Cody needs a
father."

Ah, there was the argument she couldn't quite refute.
She wanted her son to be raised with a father's love.
And Dean would make a wonderful father—gentle,
scholarly, loyal. And even though they had never been
more than friends, Elissa knew that he wanted to be.
She'd been the one keeping their relationship platonic.

"I know Dean cares about me, and I care about him.
But..." Elissa paused, trying to find words to explain
her hesitation. But the explanation was not one she
could share with her mother. Or with anyone else, for
that matter.

The fact was, she didn't feel especially *attracted* to
Dean. Not in the way she had been attracted to...

She quickly squelched the thought. She refused to
waste her time thinking about Jesse Garrett. Their one
mad night together had resulted in too much hurt, too
much shame. She couldn't understand what had come
over her!

Captain Jesse Garrett of the U.S. Army Rangers—
Dean's cousin—had unexpectedly dropped in for a visit
on his way from Savannah to Atlanta. His last night of
leave, he'd said, before shipping out for overseas duty.
She hadn't met him before that night.

When his dark, restless eyes had sought hers—and held them entranced—her world had somehow stood still. She'd never forget the feeling; as if she'd plugged herself into some kind of spiritual light socket.

*Spiritual?* she thought derisively. *You mean sexual, don't you?* How could she have thrown away all her morals and common sense just for the sake of attraction? Powerful, mesmerizing, intensely sexual attraction though it was...

She shivered at the mere memory of it. No, she wouldn't think about Jesse Garrett with his hard, muscular body and his heart-stopping stare. Or the way his kisses had incited a frenzy within her.

She took a deep breath and purged her mind of the disturbing memories. Dean was the kind of man she needed. The kind of man her son needed.

"Don't worry, Mom," she said at last, cutting into a lengthy monologue on the virtues of any man willing to adopt a baby that wasn't his. Elissa leaned her head against the kitchen wall. "I haven't said I wouldn't marry Dean."

She had barely said goodbye and hung up the phone when a sound near the front door caught her attention. Not a knock, precisely. More like...footsteps.

*In her living room.* Her heart contracted. She switched off her radio to listen. *Someone was walking across her living room floor!* But she had locked the door. Hadn't she?

The footsteps drew closer.

A shadow darkened the kitchen doorway.

Her breath stopped in her throat. She reached for the heavy iron skillet on the stove beside her. Wrapping both hands around its cold iron handle, she held it in front of her, like a club, ready to clobber the intruder, if need be. Her babies were sleeping in the other room.

Only she stood between them and whoever had invaded their sanctuary.

A man filled the shadow. Tall and broad-shouldered, with wavy raven hair. Wearing a U.S. Army Ranger uniform.

Elissa froze in disbelief. His silver-eyed stare—oh, how she remembered that potent stare—swept over her, then connected solidly with hers. And once again, the world blurred before her eyes, and all she could see was him.

An incredulous whisper tore from her throat. "Jesse."

He leaned his powerful shoulder against the doorjamb, the corner of his wide, firm mouth lifting in a hint of a smile. "I like that better than 'Captain Garrett' any day." His deep, soft, southern voice sent warmth rushing through her like Georgia sunshine. His glance flickered downward to the iron skillet she held protectively in front of her. Wry humor glinted in his eyes when they again met hers. "That thing loaded?"

It was the warmth of humor in his eyes that released her from her shock-induced paralysis. That same understated humor, unexpected in a man as ruggedly *physical* as Jesse Garrett, had been her undoing the last time they'd met. It had charmed her, lulled her into a false sense of security, deepened the damnable attraction.

"How dare you scare me like that!" With trembling hands, she dropped the skillet onto the stove. "What do you think you're doing, barging into my house?"

"What do you think *you're* doing," he responded calmly, "leaving your door open? Don't you know what kind of trouble you're inviting? That old skillet wouldn't be enough to even slow me down if I had it in my mind to overpower you."

The reprimand brought a defensive flush to Elissa's cheeks. "My door was locked! I know it was. I always—"

"It didn't keep *me* out, did it?" Jesse sauntered across the kitchen, hands in his trouser pockets, and leaned his hip against the counter, gazing sternly down at her. "Don't ask me why, but I thought you'd be more responsible."

Between clenched teeth, Elissa seethed. "Don't you dare talk to me about responsibility. You didn't even bother to—" She cut herself off sharply. What good would it do to rail at him for ignoring her letters? She couldn't change what he was. All she could do was learn from her mistakes. And never, ever repeat them.

Jesse raised one inquiring brow. "I didn't even bother to...what? Answer your letters?" She said nothing, but knew her anger radiated outward in palpable waves. "I didn't get your letters until two days ago." His tone was not in the least defensive; merely factual. "My incoming mail was held at the base. I was out on a recon mission. It should have taken only a few months, but we ran into some—" he pressed his lips into a grim line and his eyes clouded as he visualized something she could only guess at "—complications." After a pause, he summarized, "I was gone longer than planned."

Elissa peered closely at him. How could anyone lie so convincingly? She could swear he'd come straight from some hellish ordeal that he wasn't yet ready to discuss.

He *had* to be lying, though. Dean had told her about each phone call he'd received from Jesse, usually from bars and brothels in Asia. Although Dean had tried his best to spare her feelings, he'd had no choice, under the circumstances, but to relate how Jesse hadn't wanted to talk to her, or about her, or about her "little problem."

And yet here he was, in her kitchen, acting perfectly at home. Fresh anger spurted through her. "Yes, I'm sure you had a hell of a time, Captain Garrett." The last two words sounded like a curse.

"Call me Jesse." It was an order, not a request. At her startled glance, he uttered, "I've waited a long time to hear you say it, Elissa."

The subdued passion behind the words rattled her as nothing else would have. Inexplicably, she felt like crying. The man was a compulsive heartbreaker, she reminded herself. Dean had warned her, even before she had left the party with Jesse that night. Why hadn't she listened?

She drew in a breath, fortifying herself against the drugging effect of his nearness—and the unmistakable message in his bold, heated stare. He wanted her. Here and now. And though he hadn't made a move to touch her, she felt his touch and thrilled to it.

"I've been gone a long time, Elissa," he said in a solemn, hoarse whisper. "Have you no welcome for me at all?"

With her heart in her throat, she forced herself to answer by resolutely turning her back to him and walking away. She stared through the lace-curtained window at the backyard, seeing instead the starkness she had glimpsed in his eyes...and an oddly urgent need. The need for what? Probably for a quick lay, now that he was back in the States.

When she found her voice, it shook, though she strove for nonchalance. "Did you bring the waiver of parental status that I sent you? Signed and notarized, I hope?"

"No, ma'am, I did not. What makes you think I'd ever give up my son?"

She turned and gaped at him. He didn't care about Cody! What game was he playing? Her maternal instincts rose in frightened protest. She didn't want him near her baby. "Don't call him yours. He's mine."

Although his expression hadn't changed, except for a tiny muscle flexing in his lean, square jaw, he suddenly looked dangerous. Intimidating. Every inch the battle-hardened commando. She sensed an awesome power barely leashed within his muscular frame. "Take me to him."

"He's not here," she lied, praying that none of the children would cry and draw his attention. "He's away with my parents. But Cody's no concern of yours. Whether you sign that waiver or not, he'll be raised by me. Now, do me a favor, Captain Garrett, and get the hell out of my house."

Jesse glowered at her for one insolent moment, pulled away from the counter and straightened to his full, intimidating height. In a voice as soft as gunpowder, he promised, "I'll be back, Elissa. To be a father to Cody. Never doubt it." He then strode out of her kitchen.

She backed up against the refrigerator door, needing it for support. Her heartbeats filled her ears. She didn't hear the front door open or close, but she knew the moment he'd left. The resultant coldness cut through to her heart.

The phone rang. She considered not answering. She had to calm herself before the children woke. But the ringing would wake them, she realized. Reluctantly, she answered.

It was Dean, his voice unusually somber. "Elissa, I have some bad news. It's about Jesse."

She gripped the receiver tighter at the mention of his

name. "About Jesse?" she repeated dumbly. "What about him?"

A short silence followed her question. "The plane that was bringing him back to the States," Dean said haltingly, "crashed this morning. He was killed."

"Killed? Jesse? Dean, what are you talking about? Jesse's not dead. Is this some kind of a joke?"

"Joke!" Dean's tone reminded Elissa that he never joked, let alone about death. "I know it's hard to believe. I can barely believe it myself. Jesse and I grew up more like brothers than cousins. We lived in the same house as kids. We went our separate ways as adults, but—"

"Jesse was here less than five minutes ago."

Dean took a moment to absorb what she had said. "That's impossible. The military called my aunt—Jesse's mother—an hour ago. The plane crashed this morning, around nine."

"He must have taken another plane. He was here."

"Elissa, it's only noon now. Even if he somehow got on another plane, he left from an Asian port around nine this morning. He couldn't possibly have flown to Atlanta, Georgia, in two hours. A flight straight through would take longer than that, not to mention the drive from Atlanta."

Elissa's brows knitted together as she paced across her kitchen, the receiver to her ear. The army had made some kind of error, of course. Jesse was certainly not dead.

"You must have been mistaken," said Dean. "The man you saw was just someone who looked like Jesse. Haven't you ever done that before, mistaken a stranger for someone you know?"

"It wasn't like that. I wasn't out in a crowd. I didn't

catch a glimpse of him in passing. He came to my house. We talked for at least ten minutes. It was Jesse."

The silence this time lasted a good deal longer. When he finally spoke, Dean sounded troubled and unsure. "I...I guess I'll call my aunt. When was he there, did you say?"

"He left just a few minutes ago."

"Okay. Let me do some calling around. And then I'll—I'll be over there. To make sure you're...okay."

She didn't argue, although it bothered her that he thought she might *not* be okay. It was a military mix-up, nothing more.

After hanging up the phone, she paced into her living room and peered out her front window, hoping that Jesse might still be out there, walking down her driveway. After all, she hadn't heard a car pull up or drive away. He might have hitchhiked. If she could find him, she'd have him phone Dean and set things straight.

But she saw no sign of Jesse from her front window. She decided to stroll down the drive and look down the country road. Donning her jacket, she hurried to the front door.

As she reached for the knob, she halted. And stared. The door was locked, just as she'd sworn it had been. And the steel bar of the dead bolt was jammed firmly in place, securing the heavy wooden door from the inside.

An odd chill crept over her skin and beneath her hair.

The only other door in the house was in the kitchen, where she had been. All the windows were locked and fortified with immovable outer storm glass. Clearly, she remembered the footsteps sounding across this living room.

How had Jesse come in? How had he gone out?

THE FOLLOWING WEEK was the longest of her life. Jesse didn't return to her house, which was not surprising after their last conversation. Nor had he visited his family. Still, Elissa knew without a doubt that he had visited her. The question of his entrance into her home remained a disturbing puzzle, but in the larger scheme of things it meant little. Jesse was alive and she intended to prove it.

Despite numerous phone calls placed by Dean, his mother and Jesse's mother, all at Elissa's urging, the military refused to consider the possibility of a mistake. Records indicated that Captain Jesse Garrett had been on that fateful flight. His death would be officially confirmed when his remains, or whatever could be found of them, had been identified. That investigation was under way.

Elissa couldn't let the matter rest there. They wouldn't find his remains, because he wasn't dead! How cruel that his family should wait indefinitely to know that he was alive. She anxiously hoped he would come back. If not for her, then for his family.

The entire week passed with no word from Jesse. Elissa pestered her way into a conversation with his commanding officer. "He's the father of my child, Colonel Atkinson. Doesn't that give me the right to confirm his death?"

The colonel's sigh came across the trans-Pacific phone line. "The only reason I'm speaking to you now, ma'am, is because Captain Garrett's mother initiated the call. What exactly is it you want to know?"

"Could he have taken another flight?"

"Ms. Sinclair, I personally watched him board the plane that went down." In a friendlier voice, he added, "Jesse was a damned fine soldier. I'll miss him."

"But I saw him. That very day, here in Georgia."

"Stranger things have happened, ma'am."

Nothing she said shook the colonel's stand. Elissa knew in her heart he was speaking the truth. "If he was on that flight," she said, finally acquiescing, "could he have survived somehow?"

"Highly unlikely. The plane had mechanical problems and went down in the mountains. We don't believe there were any survivors."

"As far as you know. But isn't it possible...?"

"Even if he had somehow survived, Ms. Sinclair, there is no way he could have found an international airport in the area where the plane went down, then flown to the United States in the time period you've described. I also know that Jesse Garrett wouldn't have done that. He'd have contacted headquarters at the first opportunity."

Again, she knew he spoke the truth. "One more question," she asked haltingly. "When Jesse visited me, he said he had been on a recon mission. Was that true?"

At first, she thought he was going to refuse to answer. "Jesse was involved with highly sensitive projects. I'm not at liberty to say what kind of mission he was on."

"Is there such a thing as a 'recon' mission?"

"Of course."

*Of course.* Elissa hadn't known that, though, military lingo was totally unfamiliar to her. She had never heard the term *recon* before. Not until Jesse had mentioned it.

She persisted. "He said he'd run into complications, and that the mission had lasted months longer than anticipated."

"I can't say that's incorrect," he admitted, guardedly.

"And his mail," she whispered, frankly shaken now.

"Was he able to receive mail while away on his mission?"

"No, ma'am, he was not. Any communication would have jeopardized his position. His incoming mail was held here at the base until he returned."

"And that was...?"

"Two days before the flight."

A sense of unreality flooded Elissa and her head swam. *Jesse had been telling the truth.* It had sounded so unlikely—the secrecy of his mission, the holding of his mail. Which meant that he hadn't deliberately ignored the news of her pregnancy and Cody's birth.

The implications boggled her mind. Her perception of Jesse had been based largely on his failure to respond...and on things that Dean had told her. She then remembered his phone calls to Dean, placed from bars and brothels across Asia. The only explanation was that Jesse's mission hadn't begun until a few months ago. Which would mean he *had* deliberately ignored her letters. "When did he leave on his mission, Colonel? What date?"

"I'm sorry, but—"

"How long did his mission last, exactly?"

"Ms. Sinclair, I really can't give you specifics. I'd advise you to keep an open mind about that visit from Jesse. I've seen a lot of death over the years and I could write volumes about unexplained phenomena."

"I don't doubt that at all," she whispered.

"As a matter of fact, something rather odd happened the day before Jesse's flight."

She clutched the phone tighter. "What was that?"

"He made out a will."

"A will? He made out a will?"

"Yes ma'am. As if he'd had a premonition."

In that moment, the first inkling of belief trickled through her that Jesse *might* really have died on that flight...and that his visit to her hadn't been on the physical plane. As the colonel had said, stranger things had happened.

Certainly not to her.

Three days later, Jesse's mother was contacted and told that remains had been found and identified through fingerprinting. Captain Jesse Garrett was declared legally, officially—unequivocally—dead.

Even after Elissa heard the pronouncement, she heard Jesse's last words to her. Spoken with quiet passion, they echoed through her heart. He'd said, "I'll be back, Elissa. To be a father to Cody. Never doubt it."

## 2

JESSE DREAMED of his own funeral. It was one of those dreams so rich in detail that he swore he was there. Yet he knew he was dreaming and fighting against a deeper, heavier sleep.

He was back in Savannah, beneath the sprawling live oaks with Spanish moss trailing over century-old graves. The earthy smell of the river filled his nostrils, sweetened by flowers and greenery. In the beautiful but somber twilight imposed by the oaks, magnolias and dogwoods, the October sun cast dappled rays upon the small gathering of mourners.

A preacher voiced a eulogy beside the family vault, extolling the virtues of courage and patriotism. He ended with a promise of life everlasting for the good.

From a vantage point possible only in dreams, Jesse noticed his mother's hand spasmodically clutching her elder sister's. The sisters shared a troubled gaze—one they had often shared over his head when he was boy. Even in his dreams they believed the worst of him. With good reason, he had to admit. Goodness had never been his forte.

He directed his attention away from his mother, who was now dabbing at her eyes with a handkerchief. His stiff-backed aunt was next to her, her silvering head held at its usual haughty angle. Behind them stood the small knot of mourners.

The turnout at this dream funeral wasn't very gratifying, thought Jesse wryly. His mother's family had dutifully put in an appearance, along with their army of servants. But he recognized no one as a friend. No one who would miss him.

With a surprising flash of insight, he admitted that he couldn't blame his friendless state on his career. He'd deliberately avoided personal ties, distanced himself from potential friends, even from lovers. Especially from lovers. Would all those one-night stands mourn his passing when his time came? A humorless laugh escaped him.

As he tried to remember faces, only one came to mind. Elissa. But he didn't consider her a one-night stand. In his dreams, he'd made love to her every night since he'd met her.

He didn't consider her a lover, either. She'd made her feelings clear on that point. No, Elissa was an adversary—one who had a knack for whipping up his fury. Worse yet, she had control of his son. Jesse tightened his fists. Why had he built their brief union up in his mind to be anything out of the ordinary? He must have been mission-bound desperate, or just plain crazy.

At a signal from the preacher, the restless crowd began their shuffle between the graves toward their cars. Watching the assembly disperse, Jesse felt very much alone.

He'd had enough of this dream. He wanted to wake up. *Now.* Wakefulness, however, didn't come. Beckoning him instead was a deeper, numbing sleep. A forgetful sleep...

A woman slowly passed him, swept along by the crowd. She was dressed in a tailored black suit and white silk blouse. Her hair, soft and dark as sable, was tied with a black scarf at the nape of her neck and cascaded down her back in smooth curls. Her head was bent; he couldn't see her eyes, except for the graceful contours of her profile.

Jesse's weariness instantly vanished. *Elissa.*

His cousin Dean walked beside her. Jesse saw his arm come up around her shoulders. In a possessive way, he realized. As if to announce ownership.

No, he had to be mistaken. Dean was nothing more than a friend to Elissa. A platonic friend.

And this, of course, was only a dream.

As ELISSA SAT in a parlor over Abercorn Street, she felt as if she was smothering. Jesse's aunt—Dean's mother—invited everyone after the memorial service to her home on a picturesque square in Savannah. Elissa had accompanied Dean, hoping for a sense of closure, because ever since Jesse's death had been confirmed, she'd felt oddly hollow. Stricken, as if she'd suffered a terrible loss. It was illogical—she hadn't known Jesse very well—but she found she couldn't shake it.

In fact, her melancholy mushroomed and grew until she could think of little else. Jesse was gone, with no chance of returning to her life. No chance to incite all those visceral emotions that would lay and had otherwise lain dormant. Gone, before she had fully expressed her fury at his neglect. Gone, before she could understand her absolute bewitchment.

Since his death, every passing day had increased her sense that she was somehow drifting from the right path, separated from her destiny, headed in the wrong direction.

The funeral hadn't brought her closure, and looking around, she realized she wouldn't attain a sense of closure from this gathering, either. Jesse's family didn't seem to share the feeling that there was a gaping hole where he should have been. Gossipers exchanged news, sports fans analyzed football plays and business types networked, but not a word was spoken about the man they'd come to mourn. She overheard Dean chatting with a cousin about teaching high school chorus, and then her attention was drawn to the guests behind her. Someone had uttered Jesse's name and Elissa's heart was pierced by a pain she hadn't expected.

"Of *course* there isn't a casket," one young woman was saying. "After all, there wasn't actually a *body*. His remains were cremated...at least, the remains they could find. You know how it is after a plane crash—especially when there's a lot of passengers involved. From what I heard, the military had to search the jungle for...*parts*...."

In sudden need of air, Elissa whirled away. As she shouldered her way toward the open side balcony, someone clamped a hand around her arm. "Elissa, darling." It was Dean, and an elegant matron with cropped silver hair, a pointed chin and thin lips that looked remarkably like Dean's. "I'd like you to meet my mother, Muriel Pholey."

Elissa struggled to murmur a greeting as sharp blue eyes assessed her. "So, Elissa, at last we meet. Did Jesse's commanding officer answer all your questions?"

"Yes, ma'am, he tried."

"Did you know Jesse very well?"

Her throat tightened. "No, not very."

"From our conversation, I assumed you'd been... close to Jesse. You seemed so positive he was alive. So...passionate about it." Her elegant silver brows arched.

For a stricken moment, Elissa said nothing. She *had* been passionate about it. But how could he have visited her? The only rational conclusion she could draw was that his "visit" had been a psychic connection...maybe even at the time of his death. She could accept this possibility; telepathy during a trauma had been documented in hundreds of cases. But the idea of Jesse reaching out to her in distress left her aching. She had refused his last chance at making peace between them. She had sent him to his ever-after without forgiving his neglect; without welcoming him home. "I was mistaken, obviously."

"How did you know Jesse?"

"She met him *once*, Mother," Dean snapped. "Just once."

Elissa's glance cut to him in reproach. What would his family think now when she told them Cody was his son? For she intended to tell them; intended for her son to know his paternal relations. It was the least she could do to make amends to Jesse. But then, she hadn't told Dean of her intention. She realized now that he wouldn't like it.

"You met Jesse only once?" said Muriel, her blue eyes gleaming.

"Her only contact with him was when I introduced them," said Dean, looking red around the ears. "She's been *my* friend for many years. In fact—" he slipped his arm around her "—I'm hoping she'll be more than a friend." He smiled at Elissa.

The air around them suddenly chilled, as if a door had come ajar in the dead of winter. But this was October in the South, a mild October at that. With a shiver, Elissa looked for air-conditioning vents, but found none near enough to cause the dramatic drop in temperature.

Crossing her arms to warm herself, she realized that no one else seemed affected.

Muriel actually appeared warmer than before, her face flushed in patches. "Then, why did Jesse's attorney ask for her address?"

"His attorney?" repeated Dean, baffled.

Everything seemed to slip out of focus. "The waiver I sent," she whispered. The waiver of paternal status. Jesse had told her he hadn't signed it, but obviously, he had. Why else would his attorney be contacting her?

Disappointment, illogical but strong, coursed through her. So he hadn't wanted Cody, after all. Even in his last-ditch psychic connection with her, Jesse had lied.

"What had you sent to Jesse?" prompted Muriel, annoyed that she hadn't heard.

"Oh, Mother, let's not discuss boring legalities. Elissa was in the process of transferring some property from Jesse," Dean lied.

"Which property?" demanded Muriel. "That place in the Victorian section? He was forever buying old houses."

"Uh, no," replied Elissa.

"The beach lot on Tybee?"

"Really, Mother, where's your famous hospitality?" Dean interjected. "Elissa hasn't tried your liver pâté yet."

"Not the house on Isle of Hope!" cried Muriel. "You didn't close the deal, did you? Did it bring a good price, at least? That house is a historic landmark. How he came by it I'll never know. Some underhanded way, you can be sure."

"Elissa hasn't bought the house on Isle of Hope," Dean assured her. With an agitated glance around, he whispered, "But if she had, Mother, it's none of your business."

"Delia's business *is* my business," she snapped. "I've handled her assets for years." Her glance darted like the tongue of a snake toward a gentle-faced lady with white hair who was chatting contentedly with the preacher. "If only Delia had listened to me," said Muriel, "she wouldn't have gone with that Garrett boy in the first place."

In an aside to Elissa, Dean muttered, "Jesse's father."

"He *forced* himself on my sister." Muriel waited expectantly for Elissa's reaction.

But she had heard the story before—from Dean, the morning after her glorious night with Jesse. And later, when she had told Dean of her pregnancy, he had asked with concern, "Did Jesse...*force* you?"

Visibly disappointed with her lack of response, Muriel reworded her revelation. "He violated Delia. Brought shame to the family. Oh, he married her in the end—Papa insisted. But the louse didn't stay. Left Delia holding the bag—or the cradle, I should say. That misbegotten son of hers was exactly like his father. Bad from the minute he was born. He could charm the skirts off the ladies...for his own satisfaction, no matter what the cost to them. I remember the time he broke into the girls' dormitory. We had the charges dropped." Darkly, she muttered, "He sprang from bad seed. The blood of a rapist ran through Jesse's veins."

Elissa didn't want to listen. Cody had sprung from the same seed. The same blood ran through his veins. Shaken, she leveled Muriel a look as cold as the air that had grown so frigid around them. "I have to go now, Mrs. Pholey. I want to meet with Jesse's attorney. If you could please tell me his name and address—"

"Peter Thornton, on River Street," she said, "but—"

"Elissa, darling, we can't leave now," protested Dean.

"No need for you to leave, Dean. I have personal business to attend to."

He frowned, looking affronted. "But we drove together in my car. How will you—"

"It's only a few blocks to River Street. I'll walk."

"Well, if you insist. But call me when you're finished. If we leave for home by five, we'll be there around eight."

"You can go back without me. I have a friend in Savannah I'd like to visit." It was a lie, but Elissa felt desperate to be alone. "I'll take the train home."

Dean followed her to the front door. "Elissa, I know mother upset you with her talk about Jesse, but every word she said is true. And everyone who's anyone in Savannah knows it." Discreetly, he whispered, "Do you understand why it's so important we keep Cody's...ah, paternity...a secret?"

Muriel broke in, "Dean, go see what's wrong with the thermostat. It's freezing in here."

Elissa made the most of her opportunity to escape. As she hurried down the front steps into the balmy afternoon, she saw that the windows of Muriel's town house had begun to frost over.

"YOU DO UNDERSTAND, don't you, Ms. Sinclair?"

As if from far away, the attorney's voice droned through the fog that had settled in her mind. Understand? No, actually, she didn't. She'd been expecting to hear about the waiver of paternal status. So why was this lawyer talking about a fortune Jesse made during the urban renewal boom?

When she continued to stare blankly at him across his desk, the attorney explained, "To put it simply, your son has inherited Jesse's estate. His properties and his funds."

"My son?" she finally said.

The attorney sat back and removed his glasses. "Yours and Jesse's, according to the documents he signed the day before he died."

Slowly, the news sank in. Jesse had left all his belongings to Cody. He had named him as his heir. He had acknowledged him as his son. He had cared.

"He also left a tidy sum to you. According to the will, he wanted you to have the choice of staying home with Cody."

And as the attorney went on to explain about her role as caretaker of the properties and trustee of Cody's funds, Elissa buried her face in her hands and cried.

JESSE WOKE FROM THE DREAM with his teeth painfully locked. Elissa had been there with his family, letting them poison her mind. Against him, against Cody. He knew how potent that poison could be. He couldn't stop it from affecting her view of him; he had known from the start that she'd eventually discover the truth about him.

But he couldn't let the gossip affect her love for their baby. *If* she had any love for their baby. He still had to find that out. His son would grow up feeling loved, he swore, even if he had to strap him into his backpack and take him on missions.

Jesse sat up in bed and threw the covers aside, wondering about Dean's relationship with Elissa. Could there be any basis in reality for *that* part of his dream?

Had he subconsciously picked up clues to a closeness between them?

It was then, as he rose from the bed, that Jesse noticed his surroundings. The spacious bedroom with its leaded-pane windows; its polished pecan floor and woodwork aglow in the afternoon sun; the oversized Georgia pine four-poster bed with its hand-sewn quilt; the framed photo on his dresser of his old platoon gathered around a Bradley. He was home in Savannah. In his house on Isle of Hope.

But how had he gotten here?

He couldn't remember. He couldn't remember the trip from Elissa's house to here. He shook his head, feeling disoriented. Why couldn't he remember?

A sound from outside disrupted his concentration. A car, pulling into the drive. A car door slamming. Jesse peered down through the quartered panes of the side window.

A woman stood on the walkway in the front garden as a taxi pulled away. Her sable brown hair was tied back by a black scarf, with haphazard curls cascading down the front of one slender shoulder. She wore a slim black suit and a white silk blouse. In the last golden glare of late afternoon, her expression looked dazed and somber.

His dreams had never come true before, but it seemed part of his last one had. Elissa was here, in Savannah, looking exactly as she had in his dream.

A crosscurrent of emotion held Jesse in its grip: anger that she had sent him away without letting him see his son; suspicion over why she was here; and a stubborn desire to catch her up in his arms, anyway.

He wouldn't, of course. He hadn't been allowed to even touch her the last time they'd met.

He saw her graceful fingers dip into her purse as she advanced toward the front door. A moment later, he heard a key grating in the lock. *A key*. How did she have a key to his house? The only person who had one was his housekeeper.

And why did Elissa feel justified in using the key, however she happened to come by it? By God, she had some explaining to do. Jesse dropped the sheer drapery back into place, curiosity roiling in his chest. Curiosity, and fierce anticipation. For whatever the reason, justified or not, Elissa was here. In his home. Tonight.

WITHDRAWING THE KEY from the lock, Elissa paused on the front porch of the brick cottage set high on the bluff above the Skidaway River. Her first reaction to the place had been shock. She had never expected such beauty.

Huge moss-draped live oaks canopied the driveway that sloped upward from the riverfront road. The house itself, built of Savannah brick with its soft red-gray hue, its shingled roof and leaded windows, reminded Elissa of a quaint British cottage nestled in a profusion of greenery. Ivy, grape and confederate jasmine vines festooned its aged brick walls, dappled by the shade of fig trees, oaks, pecans and palmetto palms. The scent of semitropical foliage, the taste of brackish river mist and the ambience of this historic southern coastline came to her on the twilight breeze, hauntingly appealing.

This wild, soulful beauty had once belonged to a man every bit as compelling. A man who had drawn her to him with the same magical enchantment his house now invoked. Loneliness squeezed her breathless.

The place belonged to her son now. She should be gladdened by his good fortune, and by hers. But she could think of nothing but the man who had bequeathed it. *Jesse.* Her heart ached to see him, touch him, just one more time. Of course, she never would.

She knew what she had to do now. She had to make her peace with him. To say her final goodbye. What better place than his home? What better time than now?

Bracing herself, she pushed open the glossy oak door. Inside, shadows engulfed her. The heavy door creaked shut, and she battled the impulse to fling it open. Instead, she stood perfectly still at the threshold, allowing her eyes to adjust to the dimness.

She sensed a different aura than she had outside. A cool, menacing presence. As if the house, having lured her inside with its quaintness, now scorned her presence. But no, it wasn't scorn, or disapproval. It was... anger. Yes. Anger. *Against her?*

A trill of fear shivered through her, and for no logical reason, she remembered Muriel's harsh whisper. *He sprang from bad seed. The blood of a rapist ran through Jesse's veins.* Was it a lingering evil that she sensed so strongly here? Whatever it was, the presence seemed to be growing stronger. Or maybe just...closer.

*No.* She squared her jaw and stood her ground. She could not believe that Jesse had been evil. A heartbreaker, yes. But not evil. He had provided a secure future for the son he'd never met; certainly not the action of an evil man. She would not allow doubts raised by his aunt's whispers—and by her own perplexing experience with Jesse—to interfere with that certainty.

What she felt now was merely her own longing for a connection with him...and the sinister aura of solitude in an unfamiliar house at dusk.

The high heels of her leather pumps clicked purposefully against a stone floor as Elissa ran her fingertips over textured plaster walls in search of a switch.

The shadows intensified around her. A chill snaked its way down her spine. She felt that if she were to reach out through the darkness, her hand would encounter a presence, a solid presence, of whatever or whomever it was....

"Is anyone here?" she called out. She was answered only by her own eerie echo. Her now convulsive groping at last produced the switch, and she exhaled in relief as illumination brightened the room.

Again, she stood motionless.

The vast living room was floored with pinkish flagstones, the walls textured with an earthy gray, evoking a southwestern flavor. The oversize furnishings were cushioned in shades of peach, green and cream. Area rugs and pillows abounded. Luxuriant ferns spilled from hanging baskets; large-leafed plants grew near the floor-to-ceiling windows. The mirrored blinds were drawn. Bookshelves flanked a massive fireplace whose mantel was lined with souvenirs of travel: carvings of animals, figurines, pottery, bottles, artifacts and models of ancient ships.

Again, a wistfulness seized Elissa. The room—open, warm and intriguing—abounded with character. But the source of that character was only a memory, reflected in earthly trappings like these that could never bring him back.

She turned away from the living room and wandered through an archway to a flight of stairs bordered by gleaming oak handrails. Jesse had certainly had a taste for elegance. Solid, masculine elegance. She hadn't known that about him. Hadn't been given the chance. Her sense of loss sharpened.

On the second floor, she walked from room to room, the decor and furnishings barely registering in her mind. Only weeks ago, the place had been readied for Jesse's return from overseas. He should have been here. He should have been guiding her tour.

In the largest bedroom, she stopped. The handsome pine four-poster bed had been left unmade. Elissa frowned. Why would the housekeeper, obviously efficient, leave a bed unmade? Jesse hadn't returned here. Who, then, had slept in his bed?

She slowly ventured into the room. Traces of a familiar scent lingered. Jesse's aftershave, she realized. The scent activated vivid memories of the night they'd shared, when the heat of their bodies had intensified the fragrance. That scent would be forever linked in her heart with raw, carnal passion.

Had it meant anything to him? Anything at all?

Drawn to the bed, she reverently ran her hand over the pillow, swearing she saw the indentation from where a head had rested. Could she feel a warmth there, too? *Could she?*

Nonsense. It had been more than a year since he'd been home.

"Jesse," she whispered into the utter stillness, the name catching in her throat. "Jesse, oh, Jesse, why did you have to leave before I even had a chance to know you?"

And through the twilight silence of that bedchamber rang out a laugh—brief, wry, utterly familiar—that spun her heart around and sent it plunging toward her toes.

"You have a pretty short memory, darlin'" came the deep, hoarse drawl. "The way I remember it, you told me to get the hell out."

# 3

HE STOOD IN THE BEDROOM doorway, his night black
hair tousled from either wind or sleep, his skin a golden
umber from the Asian sun. His arms were crossed; one
sinewy shoulder wedged against the jamb. He wore
only loose-fitting military khaki pants, leaving his lean
waist bare and his muscular chest covered with only a
mat of dark curls. Although one corner of his mouth
curved upward, no smile disturbed the cool silver of his
eyes.

Shock drove the air out of Elissa's lungs.

How could he be here? *He couldn't be.* But there he
was, standing half a room away, wearing a powerful,
piercing stare. The same stare that had set her back an
intimidated step when they'd parted company.

"Where'd you get the key to my house?" he demanded quietly. "And why? Did you think I wouldn't
let you in if you knocked?" His gaze held her—a gran-
ite-hard gaze, yet oddly warming. "I would have let
you in, Elissa. We have business to settle, you and I."

She tried to draw a breath, but couldn't. It seemed her
lungs had collapsed, or maybe just stopped function-
ing. She'd never fainted before, but dizziness threat-
ened her now.

"Or was this your way of getting back at me for surprising you in your kitchen?" With a brief, mocking tilt

of his head, his eyes grew even colder. "Touché. And I'm not even armed with a frying pan."

She opened her mouth and drew in a tortured semblance of a breath, but it seemed to carry no oxygen. She caught at the bedpost as the room spun around her.

"You owe me an explanation, Elissa. Among other things." Through a blue-tinged haze, she watched him approach, his eyes as fierce and dark as thunderclouds. "You wouldn't let me see my son, and now I've caught you breaking and entering into my home." The very air around her changed as he neared, vibrating with his animosity.

Instinctively, she cringed away from him and his tightly leashed anger. Still, that anger quavered through her like an electrical charge. Her gasp drew air into her lungs and, ironically enough, jump started them out of their paralysis. Clarity filtered back, and she managed to rasp, "Jesse!"

"You're surprised to see me. Just what the hell were you planning to do here in my absence?"

She didn't reply. How could she? She barely believed he stood there!

His anger visibly swelled. "Damn it, Elissa, tell me."

But incredulity seeped in to take the place of her shock. "Jesse...is it really you? Oh, God. Jesse!" She reached out to touch his face.

Out of sheer reflex, he evaded her, flinching, as if she had thrown a punch.

"It was all a mistake," she whispered in soft wonder. "The whole thing—a terrible mistake."

Jesse frowned at that, and at the emotion glimmering in her sherry brown eyes. Was it...joy? Was she *glad* to see him? Foreboding filled his gut. "Is Cody okay?"

"Cody?" She sounded surprised to hear the name, or

surprised that he remembered it. "Oh, yes, yes, Cody's fine. He's with my parents. But, *you...*" She held her hands open wide, and her gaze swept over him. The unexpected welcome in her eyes seared through the armor he'd built up against her. "We thought you were dead!"

"Dead?" He'd been prepared for just about anything but that. His brows drew together. "Who thought I was dead?"

"Everyone."

Thunderstruck, he stared at her. "I've been called a lot of things, but 'dead' has never been one of them."

Despite his sardonic tone, or maybe because of it, her expression grew more solemn. "I swear to you, Jesse, the military officially pronounced you dead."

Her earnestness sent a shard of doubt through his certainty that she was, for some reason, bluffing. "Impossible. Why would they think I died after I successfully accomplished the mission? I returned to the base, and the brass promised me a promotion. Until then, I'm on a month's leave."

She planted a hand on one hip—a slim but rounded hip, he noticed. "I talked to Colonel Atkinson," she said.

That shook the sureness right out of him. "Don't be ridiculous. The colonel knows I'm not dead. He saw me off when I left the base."

"Someone obviously made a mistake."

A mistake. How could he argue with that? "Damned army," he grumbled. Another screw-up to straighten out. Dead, of all things. It had just better not interfere with his pay, he swore, or he'd have someone's head.

As she sank down onto the bed, which caused her slim black skirt to ride slightly above her crossed knees,

Jesse strode to the bedside telephone. Elissa said with an open-palmed gesture, "I *tried* to tell them that I saw you after the plane crash, but..."

"Plane crash?" He paused with the receiver halfway to his ear.

"A transport crashed on its way to the States from the base where you were stationed. The colonel swore you were on that very plane. But you...you must have taken another."

His frown deepened as he struggled to remember his flight home. A strange fog obscured much of the memory. He recalled saying goodbye to the colonel and boarding the transport, headed for the States.

And then...yes, there had been some kind of trouble. The pilot's voice had come over the intercom. Something about an engine failing. The plane had rolled to the right, and nosed down into dive. But then what?

*He couldn't remember.*

"Was there more than one flight headed for the States that morning?" Elissa queried. "There must have been. The colonel was simply confused about which one you boarded."

Jesse didn't reply. There hadn't been any other flight. And he'd never known Colonel Atkinson to be confused.

"They supposedly used fingerprinting as the method to identify your...your—" Elissa paled "—to prove your death." A visible shudder went through her. "But there's always the possibility of human error."

Decisively, Jesse dialed the colonel's number. The foreboding in his chest worsened as he listened to the ringing at the other end. Why couldn't he remember the finish of his trip home? If the plane had crashed, how had he gotten here? The questions rumbled through him as he waited for Colonel Atkinson's phone to be answered.

On the third ring, the feminine voice of the colonel's after-hours service answered. Jesse asked her to put through an emergency call to the colonel. She responded with, "Hello? May I help you?"

Impatient, he repeated, "This is Captain Jesse Garrett, and I need to make an emergency call—"

"Is anyone there?"

He gripped the phone tighter. "If you can't hear me, I'll try the call again. The connection must be bad."

"Hello-o-o?" There was a resounding *click* as she disconnected.

With a soft curse, Jesse dialed the long-distance operator, who answered promptly and clearly. But she couldn't hear him, either. Frustrated, he dropped the receiver. "It's probably this phone. I'll try downstairs."

Elissa accompanied him down the oak-railed stairway and into the living room. Even in his agitated state, he couldn't help but watch as she kicked off her pumps and folded her mile-long legs beneath her on the sofa. Her gypsy-dark hair curled around her face, tendrils dancing free from the scarf tie. She lifted worried eyes to him.

He looked away as he dialed the phone on the end table. Her beauty infused him with a tension he didn't need.

He waited, the receiver to his ear, and when the colonel's answering service picked up, he muttered a few words, then halted. *She still couldn't hear him.* Slowly, he hung up the phone. "The trouble must be in the lines."

Elissa bit the corner of her full bottom lip; a teasing thing for her to do, as far as Jesse was concerned. "Let's go use a phone somewhere else," she suggested. Her voice was slightly throaty; a detail he hadn't paid nearly enough attention to in his fantasies. "We have to talk to your family, too. They still think you're dead."

"My family." He tried to keep the scorn out of his voice. Shoving fists into the pockets of his khakis, he ambled toward her. A sudden thought occurred. "Did they, by any chance, hold a funeral service for me?"

She nodded, her brown eyes glinting auburn. "Today."

He dropped down onto the sofa beside her. "It seems I've developed a new talent." Although he spoke with self-mockery, he'd learned enough about the human mind not to doubt its capabilities. Wouldn't the military have a heyday if their training had endowed him with remote-viewing skills? He wouldn't doubt that it had. Their research and training was specifically aimed at stretching the limitations of his mind.

"I dreamed of a funeral," he admitted slowly. His contemplative gaze cut to Elissa. "You were there. And you were wearing exactly what you have on now." The spark of awe in her eyes told him she believed him. "And before that," he recalled, more to himself now, "I had a premonition of danger. It lasted days...before my plane crashed."

"But *your* plane didn't crash. You had to have taken a different flight." A tremor shook her otherwise reassuring voice. "Didn't you?"

He didn't answer. He had no answers, although he knew that rational ones existed. He was in no mood to search for them now.

Settling back against the sofa, he extended his bare arm along the seat behind her. A silky tendril brushed against his forearm, its color a few shades warmer than his own wiry black mop. He hadn't noticed that about her before—the secret fires burning in every dark strand whenever the lamplight caught it. And he wasn't sure if he had fully appreciated the creamy smoothness of her skin. Or the warmth and softness of her slender shoulders...

Jesse drew in a slow, steadying breath. His memory would return, he had no doubt. The telephone lines would clear. And this fiasco about his so-called death would resolve itself. But not tonight. Nothing could be settled tonight.

And he might never have Elissa to himself again.

Her scent, elegant and sensual, wafted to him from her hair, her skin. Gazing at her mouth, he remembered the taste of it—sweet and sultry and endlessly inviting. It had been so damned long since he'd kissed her.

He wanted to kiss her now.

The strength of the wanting stunned him. He'd felt the same the first time he'd laid eyes on her. All demure and proper, she was, socializing with Dean and his teacher friends. Too chaste and shy for a beast like Jesse. He had stalked her, anyway, with his eyes, with his wits, until he'd cornered her. But she was no one's prey. She had turned on him with concealed weapons—well concealed, brought out privately for him—her warmth and sensuality. Lord, he had wanted her.

One short night with her had barely whetted his appetite. She had haunted him throughout the long brutal months that followed, even after his mission had ended. There'd been women at the base—slim young nurses, more than willing to give him a taste of the softness he'd been missing. But he'd had no appetite for them.

He'd wanted Elissa.

He allowed his gaze to play over her elegant features,

reacquainting himself with every curve, every hollow. Hoarsely, he asked, "So...did you believe I'd died?"

Elissa tilted her face up to his, only partially surprised to find herself tucked in the warm curve of his bare arm and shoulder. He hadn't lost his boldness, or the smooth, casual way he somehow always placed her in close physical proximity to him.

Thrilling with that proximity, she tried her best to reply in an unaffected voice, but a husky one answered, anyway. "When they first told me you were dead, I didn't believe it. How could I? You'd been to my house that morning." She glanced away from him with that memory, embarrassed by her treatment of him. "But when the military declared you legally dead—" She paused, unable to explain her feelings. *Unwilling* to explain them.

"What, then?" he probed. "What did you make of my visit?"

With his warm, fragrant breath stirring her hair and his strong body vibrantly close to hers, Elissa felt foolish for ever having given in to theories of deathbed telepathy. "I didn't know what to make of it."

He studied her for a long, unnerving moment. "Is that why you nearly choked when you saw me tonight? You thought I was...a ghost?"

The last softly spoken word sent a shiver up Elissa's arms, beneath the sleeves of her suit jacket and thin silk blouse. "Of course not. I was just surprised to see you."

Silence descended around them, thick and intimate.

"Why did you come here, Elissa? To my house." The quiet question reverberated in the vast, stone-floored room.

"You bequeathed it to my son."

"Our son."

Elissa's breath caught, and the old argument between them came rushing back, startling her. She had denied him access to Cody. Refuted his right to see his own son. She'd been wrong; she knew that now. Jesse had a God-given right to see the baby they'd made together. "Yes. Our son."

"If you thought I was dead," Jesse persisted, lifting a curl from beside her ear and slowly twisting it around one long, hard finger, "who were you talking to, upstairs in my bedroom...with your hand on my pillow?"

She felt her cheeks warm. "I was saying goodbye."

He raised his brows, his eyes meeting hers. "To...?"

"To you."

A mesmerizing fire lit in his eyes, and he asked in a low, gruff whisper, "Did you grieve for me, Elissa?"

She felt it then—the slow burning away of her emotional defenses. She had no business feeling so deeply tied to this man. *She barely knew him.* But she couldn't lie, not when he'd caught her in such a telling gesture. "Yes," she finally whispered. "I grieved for you."

Some emotion flared deep within the quicksilver of his eyes, and she felt his hunger, strong and ever so seductive. "Then, you owe me, Elissa," he softly growled. "You owe me a welcome home."

His gaze forcibly held her as he lowered his mouth. Longing welled up within her. She wanted to kiss him. Wanted to indulge in the keen, sensual pleasure of his mouth, his hands, his hard, powerful body.

Alarmed, she realized she was doing it again, letting this mesmerizing stranger slip beyond her prudence and common sense—the few virtues she had left after their last explosive union.

"Jesse," she said in a panicked whispered, "I don't think we should—"

"Then, don't think," he breathed.

And with slow deliberation, he brushed his mouth against hers—lightly, reverently—from one corner to the next, the contact a mere whisper of heat across her lips.

Elissa closed her eyes and thought she'd die from the pleasure. Erotic sensations washed through her in a heated torrent, leaving her trembling as it ebbed. Trembling, hot, and wanting more. If she had doubted at all the proof of her eyes, there was no denying this. Jesse was back, and igniting a potent heat—with only the lightest of touches.

She opened her eyes, seeking him. He angled his head for another kiss, his gaze burning an unmistakable message. This would be no mere whisper.

Elissa parted her lips, ready for it. Ready to throw caution and hard lessons to the wind.

But a sudden sound jarred her. A chime. *The doorbell.*

"Jesse," she whispered, half dazed, "someone's here."

"They'll go away," he muttered against her mouth.

The next sound disproved that theory. A key turned in the front door lock. "Ms. Sinclair, are you here?" rang out a woman's cheery voice from the foyer.

Jesse's eyes darkened with thwarted desire. Beneath his breath, he cursed. "Suzanne. My housekeeper."

Still trembling from Jesse's feather-light assault, Elissa managed to call out weakly, "Yeah, I'm here."

A lanky blonde in a T-shirt and faded jeans approached them with a snap of chewing gum and a look of mild surprise. Elissa recognized her from Jesse's funeral. "Oh, there you are," she said. "I figured you were upstairs, since the light's on up there. I'm Suzanne Hancock."

Elissa's cheeks blazed with embarrassment as she rose from the sofa. She felt as if the woman could easily divine the scope and nature of the tension so tangible between Jesse and her—the sexual need that had been whetted and then left brutally unfulfilled.

Mercifully unfulfilled, she corrected herself, her good sense slowly returning.

Jesse, meanwhile, shirtless and impossibly sexy, stood up and raked a frustrated hand through his unruly black locks as he ambled toward the shadows. When he turned back to face them, his mouth, eyes and wide-legged stance expressed unbridled annoyance.

Elissa stepped forward to break the awkwardness. "I'm Elissa Sinclair. It's good to meet you."

"Looks like I caught you napping," Suzanne said with a grin. "Sorry if I woke you."

Elissa's eyebrow quirked. She thought they'd been *napping*?

With a hint of self-consciousness, Suzanne said, "I thought I'd make sure you got in okay, and give you a key to the garage." She held out a key. Absently, Elissa took it.

Jesse emitted a deep, husky sound between a laugh and a snort. "You've got a hell of a sense of timing, Suzanne."

Elissa admonished him with a frown.

But Suzanne didn't so much as glance his way. Her attention dwelled solely on Elissa, in a friendly open manner without a hint of embarrassment.

Jesse tightened his lips, crossed his muscle-corded arms and leaned against the mantel. "Hello to you, too, Suzanne. It's only been a year since I've been home."

Suzanne ignored his mocking retort and launched

into an account of problems she'd had with the kitchen appliances.

Elissa gaped at her. She hadn't acknowledged Jesse's presence by the merest glance, let alone a greeting. It then occurred to her that Suzanne should be more than mindful of his presence—*she should be stunned by it*. She had attended his funeral that very day!

An eerie tension stiffened her spine, and she looked back at Jesse for some clue to the woman's behavior. He appeared to be as bewildered as she, watching Suzanne as she cataloged the contents of the pantry.

"Suzanne," she interrupted, "I no longer need to know any of this. Nor will I need a key."

Suzanne tilted her curly blond head as Elissa pressed the key into her palm. "Aren't you the new owner of the house? The lawyer told me that your son is Jesse's heir."

"True enough," said Jesse, a hint of amusement softening his irate, almost belligerent voice. "Let's just say that the change of ownership's been postponed for a while."

Elissa awaited her reaction.

But none came. *None*. Suzanne's questioning gaze remained steadfast on Elissa, as if she hadn't heard a word Jesse had said.

"Suzanne!" exclaimed Elissa. "How can anyone inherit this house when Jesse's *not dead*?"

Surprise, at last, disrupted her calm. "Not dead?"

Elissa regarded her in disbelief. Couldn't she see that for herself? She cast an incredulous glance at Jesse, who stood with a fist on his lean hip, a frown on his mouth and an expression of fascinated puzzlement in his gaze.

"Oh!" exclaimed Suzanne, holding up a finger, her

cheeks ruddy. "You mean he's alive in some sort of spiritual way."

Elissa's jaw dropped.

"Now, that's questionable," Jesse quipped.

Bothered, irritated and just a touch frightened, Elissa snapped, "Don't make light of the situation, Jesse. There's obviously some...some *problem* here."

When she swung her gaze back to Suzanne, uneasiness had crept over the young housekeeper's face. "I'll just leave the key on the end table," she said, sidling toward the door.

"Wait, Suzanne, don't go...."

Suzanne had turned her back and now made a beeline toward the door. Baffled, Elissa followed her out onto the porch. "Please, Suzanne, I need to talk to you!"

The housekeeper beat a steady path down the drive toward her car. Tense and confused, Elissa watched the headlights flare and fade in the cool Georgia night.

A vague resentment embraced her. Why had Suzanne ignored Jesse? She obviously wasn't blind, and he'd been standing in clear view. Didn't she comprehend the monumental significance of his presence? Didn't she realize that a man—her employer—had been falsely declared dead? Didn't that warrant a comment or two?

Elissa didn't know what to make of it. Maybe it was a psychological thing. Maybe Suzanne's refusal to acknowledge his presence had been caused by denial—to protect her from a surprise too jarring. She found that hard to believe, though. If she herself had survived the shock of finding him alive, anyone could.

Wrapping her arms around herself, she shivered against the October chill as she walked back into the house.

"Jesse," she called on her way into the living room, grateful for the golden lamplight illuminating the vast room. "She left, without ever saying—" She halted. He wasn't in the living room. "Jesse?" She peered into the dining room, then paced to the kitchen. He wasn't there, either.

"Jesse!" she yelled from the bottom of the stairs. No reply from the second floor. Only her own eerie echo. "Don't tease me like this. It's not funny."

He didn't answer.

Forcing a calm she didn't feel, she methodically searched the house, room by room, shadow by lonely shadow. Her efforts proved to be in vain.

Jesse had simply vanished.

DRIZZLE-GRAY LIGHT seeped through the hotel room's blinds and permeated Elissa's fitful sleep the next morning, a Saturday. Before she had fully awakened, the events of the previous night crowded in on her, resurrecting the questions that had stormed through her then.

Where had Jesse gone? Why had he made such a sudden exit, without an explanation, without a goodbye? Those were the questions she *allowed* herself to ponder. But just beyond those lurked the ones she refused to examine—the ones that had suggested unthinkable possibilities throughout the hellish night.

As she lay alone in the hotel suite staring at the ceiling, those unasked questions imposed themselves on her. Why hadn't Suzanne acknowledged Jesse's presence? Why, when she'd later searched his room, had she found no signs of occupancy, other than the unmade bed? No clothes or shoes out of place; no coins or sundries on his dresser. His toothbrush, toothpaste, comb, razor—even bar soap and shampoo—were all stored away in cabinets. In the kitchen, the refrigerator had been void of food. The trash containers stood empty and unlined.

Perhaps he was simply neat. She'd heard that the military often instilled obsessive neatness. In her heart, though, she believed that Jesse hadn't spent a single night in his house since his return from overseas.

Which brought her to the next set of questions. How had he returned from overseas? And why hadn't he known about the plane crash, which had been on television, radio and in newspapers? Where had he been since he'd left her kitchen that morning a few weeks ago? And why, when she had telephoned for a taxi from his house last night, had her phone call gone through unimpeded?

Jesse's hadn't. The colonel's answering service and the long-distance operator hadn't been able to hear him.

Huddling beneath the covers, she drew her knees up and tucked her chin to her chest, trying to stop her trembling.

Everyone thought Jesse was dead. Should she notify his family that she had been with him last night? She imagined what Suzanne's version of events might be: *Ms. Sinclair thought Jesse was with us, but I didn't see him.*

Her trembling worsened. *What are you thinking?* she asked herself wildly. *Just come out and admit it.* But she couldn't even fathom the possibility that this last encounter had anything to do with paranormal phenomena. He'd been there last night—solid, warm and alive.

Which meant that he had been there, *physically* been there, in her kitchen three weeks ago. Again, a question reared its ugly head. How had he popped in and out through solidly locked doors and windows?

She had come to believe that that encounter had been a telepathic link with him as he died. Telepathy wasn't too hard to understand; she herself had experienced vague bouts of it from time to time. But that's *all* she had believed it to be—a reaching out from one human mind to another, with brain waves much like television or radio waves. She had never for a moment allowed herself to believe that the visit had been of a spiritual nature.

And, of course, it hadn't been. He'd been in her kitchen then, just as he'd been in his house last night, fully alive. How could she believe anything else? *He had touched her.*

Hadn't he?

A serpent-cold doubt slithered through her. He had brushed his lips against hers. Thinking back, she remembered a profusion of sensations that had coursed through her. But had she felt the actual contact of his mouth?

No. She hadn't.

Stop it, just stop it, she told herself. Ghosts couldn't kiss like that. Ghosts, if they existed at all, which she strongly doubted, were spiritual beings, with no mass or substance. No sexy smiles, or muscled biceps, or lightly furred chests. Ghosts were like illusions; holograms; vaporous masses; tricks of light, temperature or air pressure. *Weren't they?*

Of course they were. Her trembling lessened.

There was always another possibility, she realized with growing dismay, another one that she wouldn't entertain for even a moment. Maybe she was losing her mind.

She had to pull herself together. Had to ground herself in reality. Shoving her hair back from her eyes, she sat up by the bedside phone and called her mother. After asking about Cody and his teething problems, she had her mother hold the receiver to his little ear.

She felt a foolish warmth rush to her eyes. "Hi, baby. It's Mama. I love you." And though she knew that at three months of age, he wasn't actually responding to her greeting, he nevertheless made a contented gurgling sound, the kind he made after a comfy nap. Her throat tightened up. "You're my sunshine, my angel, my heart." Her eyes blurred; she knew she was being ridiculous. She'd only been away from him for one night, the first he'd ever spent apart from her. "Did you miss me last night? I missed you," she whispered.

Her mother reclaimed the phone. Elissa assured her she was all right and said she'd be home later that day, after breakfast and the four-hour train ride.

As her mother issued her usual warnings about traveling alone, an appetizing aroma wafted over from the adjoining sitting room. *Coffee.*

She remembered noticing a coffee maker on the countertop when she'd arrived last night. Had it been set to brew this morning? A lovely idea. Odd, considering the hotel had no way to know when the occupants would rise.

As she promised her mother that she'd follow her instructions to the letter, a voice rang out from the sitting room. A gruff, familiar, masculine voice.

"You take yours black?"

# 4

As the aromatic coffee drizzled into the pot, Jesse wondered if Elissa had heard his question. Probably not. Her attention was obviously monopolized by her phone call. And that was precisely why he had brewed the coffee—for an excuse to interrupt her.

Who the hell was she talking to, anyway? Her words weren't clear, but her tone and pitch were. Soft, intimate murmurs. A hint of tears held in check. The sound of a kiss being sent across telephone wires.

If she didn't hang up the damned phone soon, he just might have to hang it up for her. The ferocity of the impulse rooted Jesse to the spot. Her phone calls were none of his business, and he knew it.

*Was it Dean on the other end of that line?* Jesse shook his head in self-disgust. What did it matter who was at the receiving end of those soft endearments? Just because she'd never spoken to *him* in that tender voice wasn't any reason to feel like he'd been punched in the gut.

Dammit, she'd practically been *cooing* in there.

It was everything he could do not to go to her now and make her forget all about the guy at the other end of that intimate conversation. He could, he swore he could. He'd make her see that he, Jesse, should be the only one she would ever...

His thoughts screeched to a halt. What was he thinking? He'd be gone in a month—one short month—off to his next assignment. He certainly had no intention of tying himself to anyone, or tying anyone to him. If she wanted to whisper love talk to some S.O.B., that was fine with him. Just fine.

But it wouldn't stop him from claiming some of her time. And her mouth. And her body. *Soon.* The shortness of his leave time added a kind of desperation to his resolve.

As the coffee finished brewing, Jesse morosely reached for the cups beside the coffee maker, then experienced a profound realization. *He didn't know where he was.*

Stunned, he stared around at the room—green plaid furniture, a coffee table, a miniature refrigerator with a price list posted on its door, floor-to-ceiling draperies that most likely covered sliding glass doors. A hotel suite.

*With Elissa?*

Why couldn't he remember? He looked down at his favorite pair of faded jeans, ones he hadn't seen in ages, and a T-shirt he'd practically lived in during his last leave. He couldn't remember dressing in any of it. His memory was blank.

This much he vividly recalled—Elissa and he had been interrupted by Suzanne at the start of a kiss. Even now, his body responded to the memory. Though he had barely brushed his lips across hers, the tantalizing taste of her had been even sweeter, more intoxicating, than he'd remembered.

A question hit him squarely in the libido. What if he'd made love to her and couldn't remember it? *That* possibility was more than he could bear. Something had to be done. He'd have to see a doctor about these memory lapses.

He suspected that the problem had something to do with the trauma of his last mission. The lack of food, the intense cold, the filth of the prison, the less-than-hospitable treatment he'd received at the hands of his terrorist hosts. All this may have somehow left an effect on him. Delayed shock syndrome, he guessed, thinking of what some of his men had suffered after various missions.

As he began to unwrap a coffee cup, movement from the open doorway caught his eye.

Elissa stood there, staring at him. Her long pink robe was loosely tied at her slender waist and her white lace gown was open at the throat. Her dark hair glinted and fell in a glorious, uncombed billow; her lips glistened a smooth, natural pink. She had very obviously just risen from bed, and Jesse wanted nothing more than to take her back there.

He then realized that the glow in her amber brown eyes was *not* desire. It was anger. Incredulous anger, as if he had sprouted horns before her very eyes and incinerated her favorite sofa.

"You do want coffee, don't you?" he asked.

She didn't reply, but stood glowering at him, her fists clenching and unclenching at her sides.

With a half shrug, he offered, "Orange juice?"

Slowly she advanced, her bare feet peeping out from beneath her robe, her eyes seething. He set down the coffee cup. He'd seen her angry before, but never to this extent. Her full bottom lip was tight and a vein pulsed at her temple. "You!" she finally spat out in a tone of loathing.

Baffled, Jesse frowned. "Care to elaborate on that?"

Immediately she complied. "You are despicable.

Vile! The worst, the very worst person I've ever known."

"That's plenty 'nough elaboration for me." He eyed her in total bewilderment.

"What's your game, Jesse?" she cried. "Are you trying to drive me crazy? You left me last night, just vanished, letting me search all over the house for you."

"I left you?" *Impossible.*

"And that thing with Suzanne. Why did she act like she didn't see you?"

"I have no idea. Maybe I ticked her off. Seems like I'm pretty good at riling up women without even knowing it."

Elissa paced back and forth like a caged lioness, glaring at him. "And those phone calls you supposedly tried. When *I* called for a cab, *my* call went through just fine."

"Good for you. But how should I know why mine didn't? The lines were obviously messed up. Maybe the army's covertly taken over the running of the telephone company."

"Were the lines *really* messed up?" she scoffed, ignoring his feeble attempt at humor. "Or was that whole scene part of some scheme?" Her eyes widened at another possibility. "Is Suzanne in it with you? Are you pretending to be dead to hide from the military?"

"Don't be ridiculous."

"If this *is* a scheme, it's cruel. *And* illegal. How does it involve me?" Another thought lowered her voice by a decibel. "And how did you know where to find me this morning?" Her tone took on the hush of disbelief. "You must have followed me last night!"

Jesse could only stare at her in dismay. He hadn't the first clue as to what the hell he'd done last night.

Vaguely he remembered a weariness overtaking him; an insidious drain on his energy. But what happened after that?

Elissa interpreted his silent reflection as guilt. "You *did* follow me! How did you get into this private suite?"

Again, he had no answer. Not even a reasonable guess. And in her current state of mind, she probably wouldn't buy the truth—that he simply didn't remember. One lesson he'd learned in the military: when in doubt, keep your mouth shut.

Never had he been more in doubt.

She was circling him now, her eyes blazing with contempt. "Did you use some maneuver you learned in your juvenile delinquent days to pick the lock of my hotel door? Or did you lie to the front desk clerk, tell her we were together, ask for my room key? If anyone else tried that, it wouldn't have worked. You're a con man, Jesse. You had *me* believing things that are too crazy to even admit. I should have listened to your aunt. She said you've always had ways of charming the ladies, no matter who got hurt...."

"Ah, so that part of my dream was true, too." Anger had, at last, stirred him. "Did you enjoy my aunt's little spiel about how I sprang from bad seed?"

A fission of eeriness penetrated Elissa's anger. His aunt had said exactly that. "You dreamed that?" she asked skeptically. "You dreamed she said those words to me?"

"And what about the fact...notice, I say fact, that the blood of a rapist runs through my veins?" His voice had grown soft and harsh; his glare burned her cheeks. "She also mentioned the incident in my teenaged years when they 'apprehended' me in the girls' dorm. What did you make of that, Elissa?"

His glowering nearness forced her back a step. She moistened her suddenly dry lips with the tip of her tongue. "You...you hadn't been accused of...*rape*...had you?"

"Close." He smiled, entirely without humor. "Breaking and entering."

"You do seem to be rather good at that."

"Think, Elissa. With parentage like mine, what else would I have been doing, lurking in the hallway of a girls' dorm in the middle of the night?"

"V-visiting a girlfriend?"

Jesse halted his forward advance and stared at her. She was the only person, *the only one*, who had given him the benefit of the doubt and hit on the truth.

"A girlfriend who was afraid to say that she'd invited you up to her room?" guessed Elissa hopefully.

He shook his head, dumbfounded. "I don't understand you, Elissa. Why would you give me the benefit of *that* doubt when you just accused me of hatching schemes, conning you for some unspecified purpose and breaking into your hotel room?"

"I didn't accuse you," she protested, now thoroughly confused. Because she *had* accused him...and at the same time, hoped it wasn't so. "But Jesse, you're standing right here, in my hotel room, and I didn't invite you. I didn't let you in. Why and how are you here?"

Again he stared at her in silence.

She wanted very much to slap him. Why wouldn't he defend himself? Why wouldn't he answer her questions and give her some hope of believing he wasn't as bad as everyone warned? "Where did you go last night? Why did you leave?"

"Do you really think that I would have voluntarily left you last night?" His gaze suddenly held her transfixed. "In case you've forgotten what we were doing when Suzanne interrupted, let me assure you, I haven't." His voice roughened in a way that set her pulse to pounding. "We were about to kiss. I was about to pin you down on that sofa and remind you just what we've been missing. I fully intended to finish what we started, Elissa." His gaze settled on her lips, then rose to her eyes with bold, sensual longing. "Make no mistake...I still do."

An answering warmth rose within her, making her all too conscious of the bed just one room away. Regardless of where he'd been last night, he was with her now, and they were alone. Temptation beckoned with alarming appeal.

*Damn him!* Damn him for bewitching her so...with nothing more than softly uttered words and a heated gaze! "Are you saying someone *forced* you to leave, and you didn't even have a chance to let me know?"

His maddening, unreadable stare slid back into place. He obviously couldn't think of an excuse for leaving without a goodbye.

Her suspicions flared once again. "*Are* you involved in some kind of fraud? Do you have accomplices? Is Suzanne one of them?" Raising her hands to her head, she spun away from him, frightened by her own inability to think of rational answers. "I'm starting to sound paranoid. You're doing this to me, Jesse. Dean was right about you. You *are* dangerous."

"Dean said I was dangerous?"

"A heartbreaker, he told me. A reckless, womanizing—"

"Yeah, but...*dangerous?*"

Elissa glared. In soft deadly accents, she swore, "I've never met anyone more dangerous. You have me

doubting myself, and that's where I draw the line."
Coming to a decision—a surprisingly painful one—she
announced, "I never want to see you again. Never.
Now, get out."

"I'm not going anywhere." He crossed his arms with
arrogant stubbornness.

She squared her jaw. "Then, I will." With self-
righteous fury she stormed into the adjoining bedroom.

Jesse followed her. "Damn it, Elissa, let's talk."

"I tried to talk to you." She snatched up her overnight bag from the luggage rack. "It didn't work."

"You didn't try to talk to me. You demanded answers, and I admit, I don't have many of them."

She whirled around to face him, holding up one hand
like a traffic cop. "Don't say another word. You're not
going to embroil me in whatever scheme you've
hatched. Thank God I learned your true nature before I
got any more involved." With her overnight bag in
hand, she headed for the bathroom.

Jesse stepped in her path, his anger visibly building.
"You're forgetting one very important thing."

"I hope to forget everything about you."

"I'm talking about Cody."

She blanched. "I'd rather die than let you near him."
As she marched toward the bathroom door, she felt his
rage growing behind her.

Before she reached the bathroom, an odd heat swept
over her—a dry, invisible inferno that swirled around
her, blasting her skin, clothes and hair like dragon's
breath. And in the sudden fury of that hot cyclone, the
bathroom door slammed shut with an ear-splitting
*bang*.

Intense silence followed.

The wind ceased, but the unnatural heat grew even

hotter. Elissa stood stock-still, gaping at the closed door. *He had slammed it.* He had slammed the bathroom door from clear across the room!

Into the silence, Jesse growled, "One thing I will not do is stay out of your lives."

The quaking began in Elissa's knees and quickly spread to the rest of her body. *He had slammed the door without touching it.* Slowly, she turned to face him.

The heat, she realized through her shock, was radiating *from him.* For a moment, the briefest moment, he seemed to shimmer and waver, like a desert mirage. Then the heat lessened and the shimmering aura abated.

Fear, like none she'd ever known, possessed her.

His voice, low and quiet, shook through her like a muted roar. "I'm Cody's father, and nobody can change that."

She heard not the words, but the threat in his tone. "Jesse," she managed to whisper, wanting to calm him, needing to exert some kind of control. "Please…"

But the anger still blazed in his eyes, and he seemed fixated on one thing—whatever point he was trying to make. "You will not use my son as a weapon to get back at me for any wrongs you imagine I've done you."

"The d-door," stammered Elissa, "h-h-how…"

"A child isn't a pawn. Cody won't be used like that."

Jesse's eyes continued to smolder, and Elissa suspected he was unaware of his anger's effect—the heat, the slammed door, her mind-numbing fear. His attention seemed concentrated entirely on whatever it was he was saying.

"Do you understand me, Elissa?"

"Yes!" she cried, nodding, although her mind hadn't grasped anything beyond the fact that he'd slammed

the door from across the room and nearly roasted her
with his fury.

"Good." The anger in his eyes slowly dissipated until
they had cooled into an unreadable ash gray. He
frowned. "Why are you staring at me like that?"

"I'm not," she swore, clutching her overnight bag to
her chest like a shield.

He studied her for a silent moment, as if he hadn't
been glaring at her steadily for a seeming eternity.
"Yes," he corrected her softly, "you *are* staring at me.
Like...like I'm the devil himself."

She felt her eyes widen and her heart slow to a beat
that shook her.

She fought off the onset of hysteria. She had to get a
grip on herself.

"Elissa, what the hell's wrong with you?" The concern in his gruff voice softened the rebuke as he stepped
closer.

She dropped her bag and jumped away from him,
her back hitting into the closed bathroom door. "I'm
fine. Fine."

Puzzled, he halted a short distance away. "I'm sorry
if I yelled, but he was born three months ago. And I
haven't seen him yet."

The stark, simple longing in his eyes broke through
her terror. Was he talking about Cody? Of course he
was. Who else would he be talking about? Born three
months ago, hadn't seen him yet. Yes, he meant Cody.
*Her* Cody.

"Do you have...a picture?"

She nodded. Yes, she had a picture.

"Do you have the picture with you?" he gently prod-
ded.

Again, she cautiously nodded. Unable to move away

from the door supporting her, she pointed with a trembling finger toward the dresser where her slim leather purse lay.

"May I see it?"

"Yes. Yes, of course." Realizing he expected her to physically procure the picture, she forced her rubbery legs to move, to carry her, past Jesse and across the bedroom.

As her body resumed normal motions, her mind kicked into overdrive. What kind of man slammed doors without touching them... elevated the temperature...popped in through locked doors...vanished into thin air...couldn't be heard by phone operators... couldn't be seen by Suzanne...traveled thousands of miles in record time without a verifiable aircraft...*had been declared legally dead*....

Elissa swallowed a sob as she reached for her purse. Was she losing her mind? Was she?

From her side view, she saw Jesse sit down onto the unmade bed, his knees spread in typical male fashion, his muscled forearms resting across them as he watched her. "Do you need help finding the picture?" he offered, a frown in his dark, intelligent eyes and on his blatantly sensual lips as she stood absently holding her purse.

"Oh, no, no, I'll find it." She opened her purse and fumbled through it. Her wallet—the picture was in her wallet. By rote, her fingers sought it out and flipped through the photos until she came to the most recent one.

Jesse rose and extended his hand. "May I?" She suddenly didn't want to give it to him. This was Cody he was wanting to see. Her maternal instincts rose up in protection.

He reached with his hand—a large, long-fingered hand, bronzed by the sun; an appealing, masculine, seemingly *human* hand—and plucked the wallet from her. She watched in dry-mouthed desperation as he looked down into her baby's face—the chubby dimpled cheeks, the dark hair that stood straight up, the cola-colored eyes that sparkled in merriment.

Jesse didn't offer the usual compliments as he pored over the photo. But after a moment, the harsh planes and angles of his dark, commando face softened. A vertical groove deepened beside his mouth. "He looks like you." His soft, hoarse comment held a note of reverence.

"His chin's like yours," she admitted in a whisper. "See that cleft?"

He studied the photo closely, his concentration intense. A husky little laugh soon escaped him. "I see it."

And when he raised his gaze to hers, she recognized the glow of paternal pride...and something stronger; something that glazed his eyes with a sheen she hadn't expected to see.

Warmth blossomed within her and very tangibly around her. A strong, peaceful warmth that nourished her spirit like a sun-washed day, blooming flowers and simple happiness.

She knew then. Beyond a doubt. He wouldn't hurt Cody.

Jesse cleared his throat. "You, uh, have another one of these? I mean, can I...keep this?"

She nodded, fighting not fear this time, but affection—and attraction—for the father of her baby. She watched as his big, blunt-tipped fingers cautiously removed the photograph from its sheath. What was she to think of this man who handled his baby's photo with such tender care? Who was he? *What* was he?

"I want to spend time with him, Elissa," he said. "I want him to know me as his father."

It seemed a reasonable request. Except the fear she'd felt only moments before hadn't entirely receded. *She wasn't even sure what kind of being he was.* "When?" she hedged.

"I want to stay with him for the rest of my leave. To act as his father. It may be my only chance in a long time to...now, what's the term?...*bond* with him."

"Bond with him? For the rest of your leave? At my house?" she asked in growing alarm. She imagined doors slamming on their own, the temperature sharply rising, the neighbors talking about her invisible house-guest....

"Do you have a problem with that?" inquired Jesse.

The truth trembled on her tongue—that his unnatural powers and sudden disappearances scared her, *worried* her, made her doubt her own sanity. But before she could phrase it in an inoffensive way, a coolness hardened his gaze.

"So you *do* have a problem with that." A muscle tensed in his jaw. "Then, I'll just have to take Cody to my house."

Elissa gasped, her fear reactivating with full force. "You can't take Cody! I won't let you. I'm his custodial parent. I'll have a warrant sworn out to keep you away."

He ventured nearer, his face close to hers. "And do you think it will?"

She felt it growing again—the unnatural warmth emanating from him in waves, building along with the an-

ger in his eyes. She realized with terrifying certainty
that no power on earth would keep him away.

"A baby that young can't be separated from his
mother for very long," she explained in a frantic whisper. "I'm still breast-feeding him. He needs me."

"Then, you'll have to stay with us." Although he
didn't smile, she sensed he was pleased with the solu-
tion.

"But I have a job. A business. I can't just drop everything and leave. I'm not independently wealthy."

"I intend to pay you enough child support to give
you the choice of staying home with him. Or staying at
*my* home with him, as you will this month." His stare
grew harsh. "I'll give you three days. If you're not at my
house with Cody by Wednesday—" his eyes darkened
"—I'll come for him."

They stared at each other—he adamant, she appalled.

"Thanks for the picture," he finally murmured. And
he extended her wallet to her.

Elissa knew then what she had to do. If she were to
even consider bringing her baby near this man, she had
to touch him—firmly, solidly, so there could be no
doubt that he was, at least, a flesh-and-blood being.

Holding her breath, she reached to take back the wallet. As her fingers curled around the leather warmed
from his grasp, she pressed the back of her knuckles
into his palm.

The callused hardness was exactly as she remembered from the night they'd spent together. Vividly she
recalled the exquisite roughness—and the surprising
gentleness—of these hands on her skin. Blessed relief
coursed through her.

But before she could pull her hand away from his,
that reassuringly human contact began to change. Or

rather, her perception of it did. An odd warmth generated from the point of contact and traveled up her arm. She lost sight of where she was, what she was doing; forgot her intent and her questions. A sweet blindness stole over her and plunged her into a dimension of feeling—sensation at its purest.

Memories surged of moments they had shared, with every sensation magnified. Taste, touch, smell, sound...an intimate caress, a kiss, a smile, a groan. Snatches of conversation that had meant little at the time. Colors shone brighter, deeper; emotions ran stronger than their tentative relationship would justify. Coursing beneath the vivid sensations was a current of forceful determination, stronger than any Elissa had known. All this in a blinding flash.

But at the edges of perception hovered a curious pain; an imminent danger. A darkness pressing in, trying to blot out the brilliance, trying to foil the determination.

With a cry, she snatched her hand back from Jesse's. The disconnection jolted her, like an electrical shock. Dull red blotches floated before her eyes, as if a camera had flashed too close to her face. Gradually, her vision cleared, and she found herself holding her wallet in both hands and staring at Jesse. His palm remained outstretched, and his face reflected the same shock she had felt.

Slowly he withdrew his hand. But the pain, the darkness, was now in his shadow gray eyes. Hoarsely he whispered, "Wednesday, Elissa. My house. You and Cody." He turned, and with an odd, lagging stride, pushed open the bathroom door, then closed it behind him—manually this time.

Elissa wasn't sure how long she stood there, gazing at

that closed door. Questions, fears and possibilities tumbled through her mind as she waited for him to rejoin her. She paced through the hotel suite, the fragrance of coffee drawing her to the sitting room. She poured herself a cup and, after a few sips, decided she'd waited long enough.

Approaching the bathroom door, she called, "Jesse?"

No answer. She called again and briskly knocked. No reply. She tried the knob. The door pushed easily open.

There was no one inside.

And on the cold, white tile of the bathroom floor lay the photograph of Cody. Wherever Jesse had gone, he obviously hadn't taken it with him.

# 5

ELISSA LEFT THAT HOTEL room a woman obsessed. During her train ride back home, her teary-eyed reunion with Cody and her long, sleepless night, thoughts and questions about Jesse haunted her incessantly.

She spent Sunday researching paranormal phenomena via her Internet connection and the public library. Theories and studies answered none of her questions, or even began to alleviate the ache in her heart when she thought of Jesse.

He'd seemed so strong and vital. She didn't want to think of him as some disembodied spirit. She wanted him to be a flesh-and-blood man, in the same live body that had held her, laughed with her, made love to her. *She didn't want him to be dead.*

Was that the crux of the problem—a psychological one? Were these encounters the result of her deep-seated desire to keep him with her? No, she couldn't believe that. None of the encounters had gone the way she would have dreamed, if they'd been products of her own wishful thinking.

Monday afternoon, after her young day-care charges had all gone home, she visited the private college where Dean and she had graduated. With Cody snoozing in her arms, she entered the stately brick building that housed the humanities department and hurried down echoing corridors to the cramped office of her favorite professor.

Dr. Lehmberg lounged in her worn leather chair with her feet propped up on her neat desk. She wore a tweed jacket with elbow patches, dark jeans and hiking boots. Her ginger hair hung down her shoulder in a thick braid. Rimless glasses dominated her unadorned face as she looked up from her cup of plain yogurt and waved for Elissa to be seated.

As Elissa removed Cody's blue knitted cap and loosened his sweater, careful not to wake him, she wondered how the petite woman regarding her from behind the desk had ever managed to intimidate students without so much as raising her voice. But during Elissa's time here, few students cut Lehmberg's classes, failed to turn in assignments or disobeyed any mandate issued in the course of her teaching.

The professor's sedate gaze settled on Cody. "Yours?"

"Mine."

She nodded with wordless approval. "I heard you left Central High to have a baby. Planning to go back?"

"No." When Lehmberg's thin brows rose above her glasses, Elissa explained, "I want to stay home with Cody."

"Nothing wrong with that." She took a spoonful of yogurt. "Unless, of course, you let some narrow-minded fools run you off like a dog with its tail between its legs."

Her throat tightened. "No one ran me off."

"Think you're not good enough to counsel students, now that you're an unwed mother?"

As usual, she'd hit upon the truth. "I suppose some people might question my judgment. My...morality."

"I didn't ask about some people. I asked about you."

"I'd be happy to discuss it with you, Dr. Lehmberg, *if* you're ready to discuss *your* personal life with me."

That closed the professor's mouth. And turned it up in a begrudging grin. "Come on, now. We both know that I don't have a personal life…as far as my colleagues can tell."

The mutual glance lengthened—both women acknowledging the point and establishing a subtle new equality. Lehmberg lowered her booted feet from the desk. "If I can't bully you into spilling your guts, what *have* you come to discuss?"

"The articles you wrote about paranormal phenomena."

Interest brightened her eyes. "I've documented quite a few cases. Remote viewing, where the subject sees a scene taking place miles away. Psychokinesis, where objects are moved by sheer mental force. Telepathy, which is thought transference. Astral projection, also called out-of-body experience. Precognition, or awareness of future events…"

"But all of those involve a living subject, right? Not someone who's…dead?"

Surprise rendered the professor silent.

Shifting her sleeping baby in her arms, Elissa hesitated to pursue the topic, then cleared her throat and forged onward. "I want to know about…ghosts."

Lehmberg studied her closely, as if trying to gauge her sincerity. At long last, she queried, "What about 'em?"

"I've researched materialization. You know…apparitions."

Lehmberg nodded.

"Some researchers believe they take form from a substance called ectoplasm," said Elissa. "I'm wondering what ectoplasm *feels* like. I mean, can an apparition feel solid? Warm?" In a near whisper, she added, "Muscular?"

"Descriptions recorded of apparitions and their feel vary. But I, personally, don't believe apparitions are formed from ectoplasm. I think they're projected by the psychic energy of the departed. If the life force that drives a human being—his spirit, some might call it—does *not* cease to exist when his body dies, then I believe it's possible for that energy to project itself to the living. And to stimulate our senses: vision, hearing, smell, taste." With a slight smile, she added, "Touch."

"You mean, a spirit might be capable of making me *feel* something that's not really there?"

Lehmberg steepled her fingers beneath her chin. "If a spirit is present, then he *is* really there. How can he move things or be felt to the human touch? By the power of his mind, I say. A good hypnotist, for instance, can make his subject believe he's experiencing anything he describes. Why shouldn't those who inhabit the spiritual realm use similar methods to communicate?"

"Ghosts with hypnotic powers?"

"In a manner of speaking." Lehmberg leaned on her elbows and continued with quiet passion, "I think the capabilities of a person's spirit depend entirely on the strength of that person's mind. The strongest minds, especially when trained, can attain miracles. Like barefoot men walking over red-hot coals without blistering their skin. Masters of meditation levitating above the ground. Psychokinesis experts bending metal utensils with their thoughts. Faith healers curing diseases. Who knows what boundaries a well trained mind can exceed—*especially* after crossing over into the spiritual realm?"

Elissa sat spellbound by the possibilities. "What do you mean by a 'well trained' mind?"

"Psychic abilities are like other skills. The more one practices, the better one gets." Lehmberg lounged back in her chair, her hazel eyes brimming with curiosity. "May I ask what brought on your sudden interest in parapsychology?"

Elissa hesitated, not quite ready to share the details with anyone. "An experience in Savannah."

"Ah. Savannah. This experience didn't take place at the old Pirate's House Restaurant near Bay Street, did it?"

"No."

"One of the renovated mansions on the squares? Or the antebellum plantation house off the expressway?"

She shook her head and volunteered no specifics.

Lehmberg opened her bottom desk drawer. "Here's a list of psychical research centers you can contact—in North Carolina, Pennsylvania, California, England, Germany." She handed a page to Elissa. "Call one of them."

Grateful, she took the paper and rose. "One more question, Doctor. Do you know *why* a spirit might appear?"

Lehmberg shrugged. "Case studies suggest that reasons might be revenge, vindication, protection of a loved one, the desire to right some wrong or assuage some guilt. Whatever the goal, it's one the spirit feels passionate about. And until it's met, chances are he'll remain."

Jesse's demand rang in her memory: *I want to see my son.* Was that the goal that kept his spirit chained to this level of existence? Or was it guilt that kept him here—guilt because he'd avoided her and Cody while barhopping in Asia before his last mission? Either way, his "passionate goal" was obviously to see Cody.

Elissa paused in the doorway. "Is it painful for the spirit," she somberly asked, "to be kept here after death?"

"That's hard to say. Some spirits seem playful enough. Others, angry and obsessed. But channelers often describe a sense of anguish emanating from them. I can only surmise that as time wears on, it *does* become painful for the human spirit to be blocked from its final destiny, whatever that might be. Painful, and maybe even destructive."

Elissa knew then in her heart what she must do. She had to help Jesse achieve his goal. She had to take Cody to him.

AFTER ARRANGING FOR a licensed substitute to handle her day-care business—no small feat—Elissa faced an even more difficult task: telling her parents, and then Dean, of her decision to leave town with Cody for possibly as long as a month, with no greater reason than to "get away for a while."

As she had expected, her parents bombarded her with questions, pointed out difficulties and plied her with long, searching looks, but eventually agreed to respect her right to privacy as long as she kept in contact with them.

Dean, on the other hand, fervently objected. She wished she could tell him the truth about Jesse, but when she had casually asked if he believed in the paranormal, he dismissed it as "the silly ravings of sensa-tionalists."

Even on Wednesday morning as he helped pack lug-gage into her car, he complained. "It's absurd, leaving town on a whim. Who knows how this could hurt your day-care business!"

"You should accept my credentials as a professional counselor when I say that for the sake of my emotional well being—and therefore, Cody's—I need some down-time."

"Downtime? Okay, so I'll take a few days off and we can drive into Atlanta, see some plays, tour some mu-seums."

"Not that kind of downtime." She removed a box of diapers from an awkward corner and fit it into the travel bassinet. "I want time away, so I can think. Just me and Cody." Resolutely she slammed the trunk.

Dean grabbed her hands and held them, capturing her full attention. "Is it something I said or did? What-ever it was, I'm sorry. If I sounded put out yesterday, it was only because I'd been looking forward to your pot roast."

*That* she believed. He hated any change in their rou-tine, but especially when it came to food. He was used to a home-cooked supper at her house every Tuesday, but she'd been too busy to cook.

"You haven't done anything wrong, Dean." She squeezed his hands and gazed into his beseeching blue eyes, hating to upset him. "I'll make you a pot roast when I come home."

"But...but...who will watch our TV shows with me? How can I play 'Jeopardy' by myself?"

Aware that he was somewhat joking now with that

lost-little-boy expression that went so well with his sandy brown curls, Elissa patted his cheek. "Know that I'll be beating you just as badly from a living room in Savannah."

Softly, he said, "I hope all this thinking you'll be doing has to do with us, and that you'll decide on 'yes.'"

She didn't disillusion him, but she'd almost forgotten about the marriage proposal he'd made last month. He slipped his arms around her and kissed her. It was a pleasant kiss, as most of his were. But she backed away before he could deepen it. She simply wasn't ready for further intimacy. "Now, get going," she said, "or you'll be late for school."

Obediently he trudged toward his station wagon—a tall, sturdy figure in his blue oxford shirt, navy tie and tweed trousers already rumpled although his workday hadn't yet begun. He called from the car window, "If you wait until Saturday, I can drive you. It's dangerous for a woman and baby to travel alone."

"Don't worry. I've traveled alone before."

A few hours later, on a deserted highway miles from anywhere but dense Georgia forest, with a flat tire and lug nuts that had rusted too tight to budge, Elissa's assurance rang mockingly in her ears.

The two huge black motorcycles that rolled to a halt on the grassy shoulder beyond her car did little to allay her anxiety. Two men climbed off and ambled toward her. The noonday sun glinted on the beer cans in their hands...and the disturbing gleam in their eyes.

IN THE COMFORTABLE clutter of his own garage, the satisfying smell of gasoline and engine oil filled Jesse's nostrils; the feel of the screwdriver in his hand made him whistle a merry ditty. He'd been thinking about fixing the carburetor on this old bass boat engine since his last leave. Odd, what months of forced idleness could put in a man's head. Someone who'd never been a prisoner might guess his thoughts to have been strictly of the life-and-death variety. But his had often wandered to details he'd left unfinished at home. Like this boat engine.

And Elissa.

She'd be coming today. She'd stay the night. Anticipation sluiced through him. He'd have a whole month of days and nights with her. And he'd hold his son for the very first time. Cody.

Jesse contentedly tightened a screw on the boat engine. Life couldn't get much better.

As he discarded his screwdriver and reached for the oilcan, his attention was caught by a sound. A cry. An urgent cry. He angled his ear to the open garage door and the woods beyond, listening intently.

The cry came again. *Elissa.* It was her cry; he knew it. But it wasn't an actual cry. It wasn't a sound at all. It was a sense. A sudden, urgent awareness.

*Danger.*


SHE ROSE TO HER FEET from where she'd been kneeling in the grass beside the flattened tire. Her hand tightened around the wrench as the two men drew near.

The husky, bearded one wore shabby jeans and a dirty sleeveless T-shirt, and had snake tattoos on his sunburned biceps. The other wore shabby jeans and an open leather vest—shirtless, to show off his thin, snake-tattooed chest. Both men reeked of beer and old sweat.

"Looks like you could use some help, ma'am,"

greeted the bearded one in the T-shirt. His appraising gaze settled not on the flat tire, but on the swell of her breasts beneath her sweater, then slithered downward to the curve of her hips beneath her jeans.

"No, thanks," she replied in a voice that shook only slightly. "I've already called for help on my cellular phone. They'll be here any minute." She'd have given anything for that to have been the truth.

"Hear that, Bones?" He elbowed the lanky one in leather. "She's got one of them fancy car phones."

"I'd sure like to see that phone. Wouldn't you, Fuzz?"

A sick fear skittered through her. She hadn't locked the car doors. Cody lay inside. The can of pepper spray she'd brought as protection remained in her purse on the floorboard. Would she have the courage to use the tire wrench against the men? And would it stop them or only enrage them?

"M-my husband took the phone with him," she improvised, edging toward her car door, holding the wrench behind her, "into the woods. He had to...you know...take a short walk. But he'll be back very soon."

"Your husband?" said the husky one called Fuzz. "Where was he when you stopped at the gas station? He didn't pump the gas. Or pay for it, either."

Her heart dropped. They'd been following her...for miles, it seemed. The last gas station had been at least fifteen minutes back. Maybe they'd even punctured her tire!

"Yup, sure is funny," ruminated Bones as he pressed in closer, "I didn't see no man in the car with you at all."

Her mouth went dry, and frantically she tried to fabricate an answer.

Before she could think of one, a reply resounded from an unexpected direction—from behind her, past the rear bumper of her car, near the edge of the deep, pine-scented woods. "Maybe you just weren't looking hard enough." The quip, softly spoken, was rife with masculine challenge.

Jesse stood there, just inside the forest's shadows, his eyes gunmetal dark and deadly.

# 6

"JESSE! THANK GOD."

The stark relief on her face told Jesse all he needed to know. They'd scared the hell out of her. Anger, cold and intense, gusted from him. A sudden wind whipped the dry, rustling leaves at his feet into a miniature cyclone.

He wanted to kill the bastards.

Their progress toward Elissa stopped as they followed her gaze. Jesse stood ready for them; ready to tear off their thick skulls with his bare hands. His stare alone should have conveyed this mind-set. It was a look that had stopped fully armed enemies dead in their tracks, when he himself had been weaponless.

But these scum bag fools didn't even focus their eyes on his face. They seemed to look clear through him, the same way Suzanne had. Their eyes swept the forest's edge, lingering only on the leaves swirling at his feet.

The skinny one mumbled, "Who she lookin' at?"

The hefty creep turned his attention back to Elissa. "You're seeing things, sugar...or tryin' to pull a fast one."

Stunned by their reaction to him—or rather, lack thereof—Jesse stood motionless. Couldn't they see him? He couldn't buy that. They were ignoring him. *Had* to be...

"Somethin's whooping them leaves around, Fuzz."

An apprehensive frown formed on the skinny one's face as he watched the commotion of the leaves. "And it's gettin' cold."

Fuzz had other things on his mind. "What did you plan on doing, sugar?" he murmured to Elissa. "Running off while we was lookin' the other way?" He took a step closer and his voice lowered to a purr. "What happened—you decide to stick around for some fun with Bones and me?"

She cast another panicked glance at Jesse. "They can't see you!" Her fear jolted him into action, and he strode toward her, his anger building with every step.

Fuzz then made a tactical error of critical proportions. He reached out to touch her.

Jesse's fury erupted. He rounded the back bumper of the car and lunged, his right fist whistling as it caught Fuzz under the chin. His left fist then drove into his solar plexus, and Fuzz responded with an audible "oof."

Fuzz's head jerked sideways with the first punch. The second doubled him over. The next smashed into his nose and propelled him backward toward the asphalt highway, where he skidded on his rump.

"What was that?" cried Bones, his bloodshot eyes wide and fearful. "What the *hell* was that?"

"She punched me," murmured Fuzz in dazed amazement, shaking his head as if to clear it. Droplets of sweat and blood flung from his face like water from a wet dog.

"B-but she didn't move." Bones stared at his bloody-nosed cohort in confusion. "No one punched you."

"The hell I didn't," muttered Jesse. With another long stride, he caught Bones by the throat and wrapped his fingers around the column of his windpipe. His mouth

gaped open like a beached fish as he gasped for air.
Jesse drew back his fist for another satisfying slug.

"Jesse, stop!" cried Elissa. "You'll kill him!"

Her words penetrated his red haze of anger, and he
realized she was right. The thug was choking in his
punishing grip. With a distasteful shove, Jesse released
his stranglehold and sent him sprawling on the ground
in a gasping heap of leather, hair and snake tattoos.

The heap rolled to its bony knees and scampered
while the other thug stumbled toward the black motorcycles. Curses and mutters about a voodoo woman
floated back on the autumn breeze. Engines roared to
life. Grass flew from beneath spinning tires. Rubber
burned against asphalt.

Voodoo woman? Had they been talking about Elissa?

There was no time to ponder. A tiny sob and a
choked "Thank you, Jesse" swung his attention to
where she stood beside the hood of her car. Her face
was pale, her lips trembling. "I needed you," she whispered, "and you came."

Something in Jesse's chest rolled over. She'd needed
him. He moved toward her, wanting to touch her.

She came willingly into his arms, pressing her cheek
against the curve of his neck, her arms around his
shoulders. Her body molded to his with utter, aching
perfection.

The effect was immediate. An electric current crackled through his veins, stunning him. A tumult of emotions surged from her to him: the aftereffect of an adrenaline high; a dizzying relief; intense curiosity; profound
awe. And thick, smothering apprehension. Other emotions rushed by too quickly to understand, but packed
their wallop all the same.

These were *her* emotions storming through him,

without a word spoken. A connection beyond his comprehension. But the power blasting through him steadily grew into an unbearable force, as if to drive her from his arms.

Elissa seemed to sense his turmoil and tried to withdraw from his embrace. Jesse's resentment flared against the intrusive force. He wanted to hold her, and hold her he would. He'd worked wonders with his mental powers before. He'd bent metal with his mind, for God's sake. Surely he could tame whatever force now plagued them.

The chaos surged with an even greater strength, prying them apart. Fiercely he concentrated, fighting it with all of his might, utilizing skills he'd perfected over his lifetime. Locked in their embrace, the two of them swayed as the turbulence swirled and coursed.

It took a while, but gradually the turbulence lessened. Like sunshine after a storm, pleasure—bright and clear—replaced it. With his eyes closed and his jaw buried in her jasmine-scented hair, Jesse treasured the exquisite feel of her, the womanly warmth—sensations he had waited so long to savor again. How many times had he held her like this while alone in that godforsaken prison, or holed up in the rain-deluged jungle?

"Are you all right?" he whispered against her temple.

She raised her eyes to his, her sherry brown gaze aglow with a warmth that made him feel more intensely alive than he had in a long, long time. "I am now."

He wanted to kiss her. His gut burned with need for it. He lowered his mouth to hers.

"Jesse, wait," she cried in an anxious whisper. She stopped him with her fingertips against his lips. He kissed them, one by one...and drew the last into his mouth.

Her eyes darkened in sensual response. But with a soft little cry, she pulled her fingers away. "We can't!"

A car whizzed by them, its wind blasting their hair and clothes. He saw what she meant. They needed privacy. He meant to kiss her thoroughly, explicitly, and for as long as he damned well pleased.

Without breaking their hard-won contact, he swept her to the passenger side of her car, away from the highway, in the cozy shade of the forest. "There." His arms, strong and determined, pulled her solidly against him. How perfect, the fit of their bodies...

"No, you don't understand. I don't think we're from the same *world*, you and I."

"You knew that when we met. But it didn't matter then, and it doesn't matter now." He ran his roughened hands along her velvety cheeks until he'd captured the fine oval of her face. Gruffly, he reminded her, "You still owe me my welcome home."

An odd vulnerability lit her gaze. The claim had, for some reason, affected her deeply. And she affected him deeply. Too deeply.

With stubborn resolve, he lowered his head.

"Please, Jesse!" she cried, her whisper anguished. But she failed to specify the exact nature of her request.

So he kissed her. A slow, sensual sampling of her lips and mouth. A thousand delicious sensations swirled through him. He'd been craving her for far too long. His kiss plunged deeper then, his concentration intense.

And somewhere along the way, she lost her reservations. Wrapping her arms around his neck, she joined in and welcomed him home. Thoroughly.

The impact of that welcome ambushed Jesse. It

packed a much greater punch than the warmth, the sweetness, the excitement he had expected. Without ending the kiss, he backed her up against her car door, his hips bracketing hers. She moaned deep in her throat—a wildly seductive sound. He thrust his fingers into her hair and slanted his mouth for deeper exploration.

She broke away from his kiss with a breathy gasp. "Stop! We can't do this!"

Closing his eyes, he leaned his forehead against hers, the need to make love to her a physical ache. "I'm sorry. I know this isn't the place. Let's go up to my house."

"Jesse, it's more than that." Her breathing sounded as labored as his. "I tried to tell you, *we have to talk*." The quiver of her voice and body soothed him somewhat. It hadn't been easy for her to stop, either. "I think you're a ghost."

It took a moment to absorb her words.

"You think I'm *what?*" He could have easily countered philosophical arguments—nonsense about respect, commitment and the like. Or even indictments against his character. But this was a new one on him. She thought he was a *ghost?* In his astonishment, he allowed her to pull away.

As their bodies parted, an odd dizziness overtook him. A deep, drugging weariness seeped into his mind and sapped his strength. He'd felt the peculiar draining before—in the hotel suite, shortly after Elissa had touched him. As if contact with her somehow used up too much physical energy.

"Think about it," she said with passionate earnestness. "The military declared you dead. Your family held a funeral service for you—a funeral that you saw!

You disappear without a moment's warning. You appear in a locked suite without an apparent way in...."

Interesting points she had raised. But ridiculous. He shook his head to dispel the fuzziness clouding his mind.

Her eyes glimmered with concern. "Are you okay?"

"I'm fine." He wasn't, though. Intense weariness tugged at him and his vision had dimmed at the edges. Did these symptoms precipitate the blackouts? That's all she'd need—an unconscious man to worry about, along with the possible return of her assailants. Anger flowed within him—anger at the inexplicable ailment. What the hell was going on?

"Was it...our touch?" she whispered.

Jesse gaped at her in surprise. So she'd felt it, too. Which meant it wasn't just some psychological thing— a symptom of post-traumatic shock like some of his army buddies had suffered. Uncomfortable with questions he had no answers for, he hid his concern behind nonchalance. "At least you can't say there's no chemistry between us."

She didn't find his quip amusing. Crossing her arms, she leaned a shapely hip against her car. "Did you notice that those two buffoons couldn't see you?"

Apprehension curled through him. He'd noticed, all right. "They didn't want to see me," he muttered. "Selective perception, I'd call it." He blinked against the weariness that weighted his eyelids.

"And what about Suzanne?"

Regardless of his flip answers, the whole issue did baffle him. No one had ignored him before—ever. Even when he was a kid. They might have hated him, mistrusted him, even feared him. But no one had ignored Jesse Garrett.

"Face it, Jesse—people can't see you."

"You can."

"Well, yes." She didn't offer an explanation for that neat little fact.

"Are you in the habit of seeing ghosts?" he asked.

"No, of course not!"

"Good. I'm glad to hear that." He forced a hard little smile. "I'd better change that flat tire before I, uh, disappear." Although he'd meant it sarcastically, the statement sent an odd prickling down the back of his neck.

Elissa caught her bottom lip between her teeth.

Jesse turned away and strode toward the rear of the vehicle where the flat tire needed tending. With every step, he felt as if he were straining against a strong wind on the tilted deck of a ship.

There was something wrong with him, he had to admit. Vitally wrong. The gaps in his memory, the way people looked right through him these days. The damned shock that nearly fried him when Elissa and he touched. He'd have to take care of *that* problem soon. Real soon.

In the meantime, he wasn't about to buy into that ridiculous notion of hers! He'd have to see a doctor, plain and simple. A shrink, maybe. And he'd make an appointment for her, too.

Determined to finish his task despite the cloudiness in his mind, he wrenched the rusted lug nuts loose as Elissa busied herself with something inside the car. The tire change took longer than he expected; the weariness taxed every move he made. With acute relief, he finally bolted the spare tire in place, packed the flat one in the rear of the vehicle and turned to find Elissa watching him.

At least he could still see her. And that was no small

thing. With tiny pearls glinting at her ears and throat, in her white cashmere sweater and tight jeans, her dusky hair flowing around her shoulders, she was simply the most beautiful woman he'd ever seen.

In a solemn undertone, she queried, "What do *you* think your problem is, Jesse?"

"A woman I want so damn bad I can't see straight." He pressed in closer to peer down into her face, his breath stirring the tendrils of hair near her temples. "The same woman who pulls away from my kiss for no good reason."

A delicate flush crept into her cheeks. "Be serious."

"You don't think I am?"

"About the...the ghost issue. You have to at least give it some thought." She was flustered and he was glad.

Tightening his lips, he moved past her to the car door, feeling as if he were wading through neck-deep quicksand. "Better get going. No sense in standing here on the highway."

"That's another thing. How did you get here, to this isolated spot on a country road?"

Fighting the dimness that framed his field of vision, he opened the door for her, then leaned his forearm across the top of it. "I walked through the woods."

"But how did you get to the woods?" she persisted. "And why did you appear right when I needed you?"

The insidious heaviness was worsening, and his vision had narrowed into a thin tunnel. "The woods are adjacent to my property." He heard the slur in his words and hoped she would miss it. "I was in my garage when I heard you." Remembering his work on the boat, he looked down at his hands. They were covered with black motor grease. With a grimace, he glanced up at her. Smudges of grease marred the sleeves, shoulders and sides of her white sweater.

Following his glance, she noticed the smears herself. Her brows, like angel wings, lifted in surprise.

"Sorry," he said. "I'll buy you a new sweater. When we get to the house, you can take this one off." The thought of helping her out of the sweater blurred his vision even more.

"I don't care about the sweater. Jesse, your garage is nowhere near here. Your house is an hour's drive away."

The weariness bore down on him with an awesome weight, and he struggled to make sense of her words. "Don't be ridiculous. My house is just through those woods."

"No, it's not. Look around." Her gesture encompassed the highway and surrounding forest. "Do you recognize this stretch of road as one that borders your property?"

He pretended to inspect the landscape, but could barely focus his eyes. "Of course." Fiercely he concentrated on staving off the encroaching dimness.

It was then that he heard the cry—a plaintive wail of an infant. It came from inside the car. A smile lightened Elissa's expression, probably because of the surprise that must have crossed his features. She leaned into the car and reached into the back seat.

Realization hit Jesse like a bucket of cold water. *It was Cody. Cody was here, in the car.* He had asked her to bring him, but in the commotion of the fight—and then the heat of their kiss—he hadn't given the baby a thought.

He bent to peer around Elissa, trying to see his son. His vision had blurred so much, he could make out only vague outlines.

Elissa soon emerged from the car, her face very near his as she gazed up at him in the narrow door opening. "He lost his pacifier," she explained, her voice hushed.

"He's already back asleep. He fussed the first couple hours of the trip, so he should sleep awhile longer."

A ground swell of emotion lifted Jesse's heart. His son was here; the child born from the love Elissa and he had shared. He wanted to pull the front seat forward to see him better, but the weariness had grown too heavy to hold off.

He had to leave her, had to be alone. He didn't stop to analyze the need; it was too urgent, too basic. Clenching his teeth, he said with an effort, "I'm going up to the house. Meet me there." He turned and headed for the woods.

"But your house is an hour's drive away from here!"

"It's just around the bend." He didn't break his stride, but a disturbing question occurred to him. If he had actually passed out during those lapses in his memory, why hadn't Elissa found him lying somewhere? He'd been in his own house the first time, in her hotel suite the second. Even if he'd wandered away before succumbing to unconsciousness, surely someone would have found him.

"Jesse!" wailed Elissa. "Come back!"

From the cool shadows of the forest, he called, "I'm going home to clean this grease off my hands." He forced a smile into his next words. "I plan on holding my son."

*And you. Through a whole month of nights.* No force on earth would stop him.

ELISSA COULDN'T QUITE bring herself to drive away from the roadside spot. How could she leave him without a ride home?

Silly, she knew. He had appeared out of nowhere, and would apparently go back the way he'd come. The problem was making herself believe it.

How could a ghost kiss like that? How could their bodies fit together with such perfection? In the space of a few thunderous heartbeats, he'd swept her away to a dimension of pure sensual longing. No man in her entire life had ignited her passion so quickly, so fiercely—except Jesse. She remembered the last time he'd kissed her, the night she had thrown a lifetime of scruples to the wind and made love with a perfect stranger. His kiss hadn't changed, not one iota.

So how could he be a ghost?

When she finally forced herself to pull back onto the highway and resume her journey, she almost expected his house to be "right around the bend," as he had predicted. But it wasn't. Her map plainly indicated that the nearest town was a good sixty miles away from his home on Isle of Hope.

So how could he *not* be a ghost?

The questions went on and on. When she stopped in Savannah to grab a sandwich, feed Cody and change his diaper, she looked down at her sweater and suffered another surprise. It was clean, without the slightest smudge of grease. But she had seen the black smears with her own eyes....

Elissa thought about Dr. Lehmberg's theory. If strong-minded spirits could stimulate the human senses, make one see, taste, smell, hear and feel things that might not actually be taking place, was this the case with Jesse? Virtual reality?

She leaned her head back against the headrest and closed her eyes. The heat of his embrace, the thrill of his kiss, the passion he incited, had surely felt like reality. He had made *her* feel truly alive.

She pulled into the oak-canopied driveway of Jesse's home on the river bluff and looked at her watch. One-thirty—one hour since their roadside tryst.

His house, with its red-gray Savannah brick festooned with vines, its quaint shingled roof and leaded windows, stood quiet and dark beneath the profusion of exotic, semitropical trees. Holding Cody tightly in her arms, Elissa ventured up the front steps to the glossy oak door and pressed the doorbell.

Chimes echoed within. A mournful, lonely sound.

No one answered.

Her heart sank. Where was he? With the key his attorney had given her, she unlocked the massive door and found the place exactly as she had left it—cool and vacant. No food in the refrigerator, no trash in the trash container, no clothes in the hamper, no toiletries out of place. The house had obviously not been lived in for a very long time.

*Of course not,* she chided herself. *Its owner is dead.* Anguish struck her anew. What had she expected—a fire in the hearth, a meal on the stove? It occurred to her that she had no guarantee even of his company. He might not return.

Had he disappeared because their kiss had robbed him of vital energy? Although he had tried to hide the weariness, she had seen it overtake him, just as it had in the hotel room. Had he disappeared in the solitude of the forest? Again, their contact had been her fault; she had lunged into his arms without thinking. Would he come back this time?

Squaring her jaw, Elissa resolved to buck up and adopt an optimistic outlook—Jesse would return. Allowing herself no idle time to entertain doubts, she busied herself settling in. She unpacked her luggage and set up Cody's travel crib in the bedroom across from Jesse's. She stacked firewood on the stone hearth for an evening fire. She drove to the nearest grocery store and stocked the kitchen with food. All the while, she listened for Jesse's footsteps, bracing herself for his sudden appearance.

Jesse did not appear that day, or the next.

With his house dark and brooding around her on that second night, she readied herself for bed, struggling to maintain her optimism. Not an easy task. Jesse hadn't had the chance to hold Cody, or to even get a very good look at him. Had he gone to his ever-after without accomplishing his final mission? What sad irony for a proud soldier.

She wanted to pray, but wasn't sure what to pray for.

She truly did want the best for Jesse, whatever that might be. Yet she had to admit that she also wanted to see him again. At least one more time.

Sleep eluded her. As midnight struck, she lay peering into the bedroom shadows, searching the darkness for movement, wondering whether shadows walked the halls this night. She shivered beneath the bedcovers, very much afraid—not that the house was haunted, but that it was not.

Her fear took an entirely different turn in the morning. It grabbed her heart with icy hands and squeezed tight. When she had reached into the small crib near her bedside, she had found that it was empty.

# 7

SHE TORE MADLY through the house, from room to room, her heart thundering, her fears ranging from common everyday kidnapping to vengeful spirits. She clung to the hope of something in between. She prayed that Jesse had returned and would be waiting downstairs with Cody safe in his arms.

No one awaited her downstairs, or in any other room of the house. Fear pounded through her as she stopped her wild pacing in the center of the vast living room, trying to marshall her thoughts and form a plan.

That's when she heard it—the low murmur of a voice coming from the back yard. Behind the mirrored vertical blinds, the sliding glass door to the walled garden had been left slightly open. With her heart in her mouth, she edged toward that garden door and drew the blinds aside.

There he was, the kidnapper. The vengeful spirit.

With his bare back against a muscular, T-shirted chest, his diapered rump supported by one large sun-bronzed hand, a huge thumb supporting his drool-shiny chin, and gigantic fingers splayed down the length of his pinkish, chubby body, Cody blew spit bubbles, kicked his dimpled legs and gazed around the garden with bright-eyed contentment.

Unaware of his adult audience, Jesse turned the baby toward a particularly lovely tree between the terra-cotta stucco wall and a small wrought-iron gate. "And *this*," he instructed, "is a tea olive. You smell that?" He inhaled through his nose with dramatic vigor—obviously so that Cody would catch on and do the same. "Mmmm. Nothing in the world smells better than that, son. Except a woman's hair and skin. But you've got quite some time before you'll know about that." He stepped toward the tile-bordered pool, where tiny jets of water stirred the lily pads. "And over here..."

Jesse stopped in the center of the courtyard, his gaze lighting on Elissa, who watched him from the doorway. A corner of his mouth quirked up into a grin, and his eyes greeted her with all the warmth of the Georgia morning sun.

A smile tugged at her lips, fright replaced by giddy relief—and another tender emotion that she dared not name.

"And over here," he said, "we have this lady we call your mama." His leisurely gaze took in all of her—her uncombed hair, her unmade-up face, her long pink nightgown that was neither attractive nor revealing. She tossed her tangled curls behind her shoulder, crossed her arms and pretended not to care that she looked her absolute worst.

Jesse continued with his tour-guide approach to parenting. "This lady, who's finally graced us with her presence, is not only your mama, but one heck of a kisser. You ever hear of a woman kissing a man senseless? Probably not. But this woman can. Not that it's any of your business, son. It's my business." Jesse ambled closer, his voice taking on a husky quality, his gaze descending to her lips. "And I plan to tend to it, soon as possible."

Elissa felt her cheeks warm and glanced away from

his hypnotic silver gray eyes. "Time for a diaper change."

"His diaper's already been changed." Jesse planted a kiss on top of the baby's head, where dark, wispy hair stood up in all directions above bright, cola-colored eyes. Cody looked so tiny and fair in Jesse's virile, sun-tanned arms—but in many ways, the resemblance between the two was uncanny. The arc of their eyebrows, the cleft of their chins, the shape of their mouths and noses.

"You changed his diaper?" Elissa asked in surprise.

"Yes, ma'am. And it was a nasty one, too."

She gaped disbelievingly. "Where and how?"

He raised one arrogant brow. "Oh, ye of little faith. You think I don't know how to take care of my own son?" When her unrelenting gaze pressed for an answer, he said, "I took him out back and hosed him off."

Elissa gasped. "You washed his bare little bottom with cold hose water?"

A frown protested her slant on the incident. "The weather's nice. In fact, by eight-thirty, it was warm as all he—" he paused, glancing down at his son "—as all *heck* out here. At least eighty-five degrees." Elissa had to admit, the weather was unseasonably warm. "He might have been a little surprised at first," Jesse allowed, "but he's a staunch little soldier." His gaze dropped to Cody with paternal pride. "He's got that Garrett blood in him."

Elissa rolled her eyes, stepped barefoot into the stone-floored courtyard and took the happily gurgling baby from Jesse's arms. Critically, she inspected his job of diapering. He had certainly made an elaborate production out of it. Intricate tucks and folds fitted the diaper with tailored perfection to Cody's bottom—not a gap or uncomfortable wrinkle anywhere in sight. Of course, he *had* used every one of the dozen pins from the diaper bag to accomplish this feat. Nevertheless, it was a truly impressive finished product.

"You kept him still enough to do...all this?"

"He had his rubber duck to gnaw on."

Her lips curved with suppressed laughter. "You found Mr. Duckie?"

He bent her a quelling glance. "A man's got to do what a man's got to do."

She nodded, her eyes bright with merriment. "You did a fine job, Captain Garrett." With her free hand, she saluted him. He looked inordinately pleased at the compliment. "What did you do with the dirty diaper?"

"What else? I trashed it."

"But that was a cloth diaper."

He shrugged. "I'll buy him more. As many as he needs."

Elissa stared at him. Could this possibly be the same man who had called Dean from a brothel in Asia and said he didn't want to hear about her "little problem"?

The old doubts came fluttering back. Was this lavish show of fatherly concern merely for her benefit—to make her fall into his bed during his month's leave? Elissa pulled herself up short. What was she thinking? This wasn't a man standing beside her; it was a *ghost*. She mustn't forget that. He hadn't hung around this mortal plane just to get her into the sack. It was Cody he had stayed for.

It then became quite clear just what Jesse's final objective was—to make up for his earlier, callous neglect. He apparently hadn't developed his parental conscience until it was too late. Postmortem.

His timing ticked her off.

She tried to soothe herself with the fact that he had named Cody in his will. On the other hand, if he'd really experienced a premonition of death, as both Colonel Atkinson and Jesse himself had told her, that little legality might have been a last-ditch effort to ease himself through judgment day.

Peeved, she hugged Cody tighter and turned to seek the privacy of the bedroom. "Time for your breakfast, angel," she murmured against his soft, rounded cheek.

"Great," said Jesse. "I'm starved."

"Not you."

"Oh." He shot her an irrepressible grin. "Then, I'll just watch."

"Cody prefers to breakfast in private, thank you." As she made a move toward the doorway, she stopped with a sudden thought. "Jesse, when you and I touched, we both felt something. It was as if we...shouldn't be touching."

He leaned a broad shoulder against the doorjamb and frowned down at her. "I felt the shock, but I wouldn't jump to *that* conclusion about it."

"Did you feel it when you touched Cody?"

"No, of course not. It wasn't that kind of touch."

Her brows rose. "You think it happens to us because of something...sexual?"

His voice lowered an octave, and his eyes turned a smoky gray. "Don't you?"

"No, I don't." She hoped her sudden flux of body heat wasn't visibly apparent. "When I touched you in the hotel suite, I hadn't been thinking about sex."

A roguish smile lit his eyes. "Maybe *you* weren't."

"Jesse, this isn't a joking matter!"

"And I wasn't joking." His gaze drove home that point. A tension-filled silence ensued. After a moment, he quietly asked, "How long did it take you to get here?"

Although his tone hadn't actually changed, Elissa sensed a sudden sobriety in it. She knew he meant from the location of their roadside meeting. "A little over an hour."

He said nothing, but she could see the news stunned him.

"Where were you since then?" she asked.

"I don't know." He stared at her in perplexity. "I found you in bed sleeping, so I assume our roadside visit occurred...yesterday?"

She shook her head.

"Couldn't have been today. It happened around noon, I'd say, judging from the sun...."

"Noon, yes. Two days ago. That was Wednesday," she reminded him. "Today's Friday."

Every trace of Jesse's former joviality vanished. "I'll go find us something for breakfast," he finally murmured, "while you feed Cody. We need to talk."

"SO WHAT DO YOU MAKE of all this, Jesse?"

They were sitting in the dappled shade of the quaint walled garden, a basket of buttermilk biscuits, a bowl of fresh strawberries and mugs of coffee all but forgotten on the glass-topped table between them.

Cody had fallen asleep in his windup swing as Jesse told Elissa about his memory lapses. They had discussed the fact that no one seemed able to see him or hear him except her; they pondered his ability to answer her silent call for help from many miles away; they commented on the strange circumstances surrounding his flight home from overseas. She also reminded him that the government had declared him dead—the fact that carried the least weight with Jesse.

"If only I could remember what happened after the plane went down. It rolled to the right, then angled into a nosedive...." He squinted in an effort to concentrate. After a few moments, he shook his head. "Then nothing," he reported glumly. "I can't remember a damn thing after that."

"So you're sure you were on the plane that crashed?" She heard the disappointment in her own voice. In her heart of hearts, she'd still been hoping for some bizarre mistake.

His lips tightened into a grim, white line. "No doubt in my mind." A plethora of unasked questions hovered between them. "You really do think I'm a...ghost... don't you?"

It had been difficult for him to say the *g* word, she knew. It was difficult for her to say it, too. "Can you think of any other explanation?"

"Of course."

Hopefully, she waited.

"Some crazy Asian medical syndrome, obviously."

Her hope again died. "A medical syndrome that makes you invisible to everyone but me?" She sat back in her chair and raked a clump of wayward curls from her forehead. "If you think that's it, why haven't you called a doctor?"

"I did. The receptionist couldn't hear me."

"Funny, the phone's been working fine for me." She couldn't help the sarcasm. "Dean called me just last night."

Jesse frowned. "Dean?"

"Your cousin, remember?"

"Of course I remember. Why was he calling you here?"

"Just to check up on me. Make sure I'm okay."

"Why the hell wouldn't you be? You're in my home, with me."

"Jesse, don't you understand? He thinks you're dead. Everyone thinks you're dead." She flattened her palms on the table and leaned forward, her dark eyes bright and earnest. "*I* think you're dead."

"That's a hell of a thing to say. I serve you biscuits, brew your coffee, and what thanks do I get? 'Jesse, I think you're dead.'"

"Stop joking about it," she reprimanded him sharply. "It's true. *You are dead.*"

Silence followed her outburst.

Jesse leaned back in his chair, folded his arms and studied her. She wasn't crazy; he knew that. And she truly believed what she was saying. If he were to be honest with himself, he'd admit she had some good reasons to believe as she did. But his years of covert military experience had taught him to look beyond any explanation that didn't sit well in his gut. Her explanation weighed far too heavy there. "You're a peculiar woman, Elissa."

She threw her hands up and fell back against her seat. "And you're a stubborn man, Jesse Garrett."

He stroked his beard-stubbled chin. Things could be a lot worse, he reflected. Elissa was here, with his son, to stay for at least a month. He cocked her a tentative smile. And after a few moments of stubborn resistance, she grudgingly gave in and answered his smile with a slight one of her own.

Squeaks from the windup swing and an exuberant

squeal diverted their attention from each other to Cody—wide-eyed, kicking and ready for fun.

Elissa reached for him, her smile now so radiant that Jesse's throat constricted. No matter what pain and sacrifice the baby's existence had caused her, she loved the little tyke with the kind of love that could bring only happiness. That kind of love Jesse himself had never known. He'd been an embarrassment to his own mother, proof of a wrong done to her, a social blight. Elissa could have so easily felt the same about Cody. But she did not.

A deep tenderness welled up in him, not only for the baby boy who shared his blood, but for the woman who so obviously treasured him. With playful zest, she plucked Cody out of the swing and nuzzled his neck, making him laugh and squeal with delight. She laid him in her nightgown-clad lap, cooed at him, growled against his tummy, played "patty-cake, patty-cake, baker's man."

Her thick, dark hair was tangled, her pink gown was an oversize T-shirt, her face betrayed distinct laugh lines in the morning sun. He'd never seen a woman he wanted more in all his life.

"And do you know who that is, over there?" She stood Cody up in her lap, facing Jesse, and spoke against his pudgy little cheek. "That's your Dada."

"Dada?" repeated Jesse in surprise.

Her cheek dimpled. "Yes, Dada. Can you say that, Cody? Da-da-da?"

And though Jesse managed a creditable smirk—as if he objected to the infantile form of address—his heart swelled beyond capacity. She was including him in their family circle. More than that—she was acknowledging his place at its very heart. She could have paid him no finer tribute; given no finer gift. He could have wept with the joy of it.

But weeping wasn't his style. He swallowed—admittedly hard—and reached out a finger for Cody to wrap his little hand around. "Give me a shake, there, boy. A handshake for your old pa." He saw Elissa's brows rise in response to his preferred title. "Can you say that? Papa-pa?"

He had watched Cody reach for Elissa's fingers during their play. He had watched his face light up in response to her smile. But as Jesse leaned across that table, waving his finger in the baby's plain view, Cody did not reach out. His eyes didn't even focus on the finger...*or on Jesse's face.*

A bone-deep chill seeped through him. With slow deliberation, he waved his hand in front of the baby's eyes. Cody didn't so much as blink.

"He can't see me." Jesse turned his gaze to Elissa.

The bleakness there tore at her heart. She wished she could tell him he was wrong. She wished she could make it not so. But she knew from Cody's lack of response that Jesse wasn't mistaken.

The stricken look remained for only a very short time before a familiar determination hardened Jesse's eyes to a granite gray. "Get your car keys, Elissa. And Cody's stroller."

"Why? Where are we going?"

"Into town. I think it's time I do a little investigating about this condition of mine."

THE EXCURSION STARTED out predictably enough. They drove into the historic section of Savannah, where Elissa pushed Cody in his stroller down the bricked

pathways of lush green squares and on sidewalks past
restored historical homes, inns and shops.

Jesse, for the most part, walked with them. But it had
been immediately apparent, from the moment he'd
climbed from Elissa's car and greeted a young couple
jogging by, that no one else could hear or see him.

Things only got worse from there.

He waved his hand in people's faces and marveled
when they failed to react. He tapped a fashionably at-
tired businessman on the shoulder and asked for the
time. The man turned and lifted his brows at an elderly
woman, who marched by with a righteous tilt of her
head and girlish blush on her weathered cheeks. Jesse
scolded a purple-haired teen for having too many gold
studs in her nostrils—"I like my women with one. Two,
at the very most." The girl slinked on without so much
as a scowl.

Even that wasn't enough for Jesse. He lifted a cap
from a kid's head and set it on his little sister, which in-
stigated a loud altercation. He caught a ball that another
boy had been tossing up into the air. The boy gaped at
the ball Jesse held, then tugged at the woman in front of
him. "Look, Mom, look! My ball's stuck in the air!" She
absently patted the boy on the head and continued her
conversation with the woman beside her.

Elissa couldn't help but intervene at that point.
"Jesse!" she admonished from a few yards away. With
a sheepish grin, he tossed the ball back to the boy, who
examined it with wide-eyed reverence.

Jesse returned to Elissa's side and escorted her across
a shady street toward a sidewalk café. "It's the
damnedest thing I've ever seen," he muttered. "They
can't see me, they can't hear me, but they can feel my
touch."

Elissa had to bite her tongue to keep from asking what he felt when he touched them. People sat at outdoor umbrella tables, casting her casual glances and brief smiles for the baby. What would they do if she started talking to an invisible man? Cart her off to a padded cell, that's what.

"What do you think would happen," mused Jesse, "if I blocked their way? Would they bump into me?"

Foreboding shivered through Elissa. "Don't try it!"

The plea drew the attention of ladies seated at a nearby umbrella table. She looked down at Cody and, in a rush of embarrassment, stuck the pacifier into his mouth. "Don't...don't throw your pacifier again, sweetie, or we might not find it this time."

Cody accepted the pacifier in sleepy contentment as Elissa wheeled him beyond earshot of the sidewalk café.

Beside her, Jesse muttered, "I have to know what I'm dealing with here." And with his thumbs hooked in the pockets of his tight, faded jeans, he stepped into the path of an oncoming crowd.

Elissa flinched as a long-haired, husky youth with headphones walked into him. But there was no collision. The youth, and the crowd behind him, walked on without interruption. Elissa heard a woman remark, "Oh, do you feel that chill? I'll bet we're in for some rain." Her companion mumbled in agreement.

Elissa stood with her fingers wrapped tightly around the stroller bar, staring in dry-mouthed horror. Jesse was gone. Gone! Vanished in the midst of that crowd.

"Jesse?" she whispered when the crowd had passed.

No one answered.

With shaking knees, she forced herself to stroll to the end of the block, casting hopeful glances around the city streets, praying to see Jesse among the pedestrians. Where had he gone? What had happened to him? Had he broken some cardinal rule of the spiritual realm, damning him to some netherworld for all eternity?

*Oh, Jesse. Please come back.*

But he didn't.

She returned to his house alone, her stomach knotted, her nerves frazzled, her hopes set on something she knew to be foolish. Why *should* he return? If his unresolved goal had been to see and hold Cody, he had accomplished it. And by bequeathing his house and money to Cody, he had provided for his future, as well. What more could the most conscientious ghost hope to accomplish in regards to his son?

This earthly plane was no place for Jesse anymore. It was right for him to move on to whatever his destiny held in store, Elissa told herself. He belonged elsewhere.

It was only her heart that begged to differ.

HE WAKENED TO the chirping of crickets, the humming of insects and the croaking of frogs, with the scent of autumn grasses and river mist heavy on the cool October night air. His first inclination was to listen for movement: voices, footsteps, faraway gunfire.

But by the dim light of a hazy crescent moon, he quickly recognized his surroundings—the driveway of his home, not a riverbank in some foreign thicket. And though he had just wakened, he found himself not lying down, or even recumbent against some tree, but walking with cautious, determined strides, as if on patrol.

Jesse frowned. Where the hell had he been since this afternoon? He remembered his trip to town with Elissa

and his experimentation there. He remembered standing in the path of an oncoming crowd. Then what?

Nothing. A total absence of memory.

What had they done to him? What the *hell* had the
military done to him now? He'd gone along with their
psychic experiments, submitted to their testing, honed
his mental powers into a viable force that had won
them success in situations that would have otherwise
proved impossible. He had bent metal with his mind
for them—freeing hostages from terrorists' prisons,
jamming weapons that would have otherwise destroyed cities, disabling enemy aircraft at the most cru-
cial of times. Yes, he had allowed the military to
strengthen his mental powers with methods their researchers had perfected.

But he had always drawn the line at drug experimentation or anything that could physically affect him. Had
they tried some new drug or technology on him without his knowledge? Was *he* their guinea pig—their new-
est weapon?

He clenched his fists in fury. What else could explain
his condition? He strode up the driveway, his footsteps
crunching like so many necks breaking. He'd find out
who was behind this, he swore, and he'd make them
sorry.

Questions flashed through his mind at rapid-fire
pace. Why had they allowed him to leave? Had they really intended to set him loose in a civilian setting? Did
they know where he was, or were they searching for
him now?

Doubts whispered through him.

Elissa had said she called the colonel and told him of
his first visit. If the military was conducting some bizarre experiment with him, why hadn't the colonel be-

lieved that she saw him? Why hadn't he asked for the
details and sent someone to follow up? Common sense
answered that question: because the colonel thought he
was dead.

The puzzle pieces didn't fit. Jesse didn't like it.

Forcing his anger to subside, he climbed the steps to
the front porch. He couldn't afford the luxury of anger.
He had to keep a clear mind if he hoped to find the
truth.

He tried the door and found it locked.

Elissa's car was still in the driveway, he noted. Which
meant she was here. He wanted badly to see her; *needed*
to be with her. She was his sanity in a world that had
ceased to make sense.

Checking the pockets of his pants and shirt for his
keys, Jesse realized he was wearing his army fatigues.
He also realized he had no key. With a muttered curse,
he lifted his hand to knock, then stopped. Hadn't Elissa
accused him of appearing in locked rooms without an
apparent way in? He stared at the door for a doubtful
moment. What would happen if he...?

Taking a step back, he braced his shoulders, covered
his head with his arms and forged slowly, steadily, onward. He fully expected the heavy oak barrier to stop
him.

He encountered no barrier.

Lifting his head, Jesse found himself inside.

The magnitude of this discovery—and all the others
he'd made today—washed over him in icy waves.
Whatever the cause, he was no longer a normal, flesh-
and-blood man. He was something quite, quite different. Would this difference be...permanent?

Determination tightened the muscles of his jaw. He
could not allow that. He would diagnose the exact na-

ture of the problem and take whatever measures were necessary to correct it. Strengthened by his resolve, he glanced around the darkened living room. Elissa was obviously upstairs.

He took the steps two at a time.

When he reached the upper corridor, he paused in the open doorway to her bedroom. The only light spilled from the door left slightly ajar to the adjoining bath. The bed was neatly made, with no one sleeping in it.

He'd been hoping to find her there.

The rhythmic breathing of the baby in the crib drew Jesse to the far corner, where he gazed down at his slumbering son. "I promise you, Cody, you'll grow up with a father," he vowed. "A real father."

The gentle swoosh of water and the slurp of a drain lifted Jesse's head toward the bathroom door. Elissa, it seemed, had been bathing. His anticipation sharpened into hunger. He wanted to see her. Touch her. Renew his soul, his life force, by making long, hard love to her.

The bathroom door slowly opened and blossom-scented steam wafted out. The bathroom light flicked off, pitching the bedroom into an even deeper darkness, relieved only by a night-light near the bed.

Quietly she tiptoed, her hair wet, her skin dewy, her slender body wrapped in only a thin white towel, fastened by a tuck between her breasts. She didn't immediately notice him, but headed for the baby's crib, where she peered down at the sleeping infant.

"Our stroll must have worn you out," she whispered, adjusting the blanket around him with a tender smile. "It's past your feeding time." She then turned and reached for her pink nightgown, which lay draped across an armchair.

Jesse caught hold of the nightgown first, and whisked it sufficiently beyond her reach.

# 8

THE NIGHTGOWN FLEW OUT of her hand, startling her.

A figure loomed in the shadows, then materialized in the dim light—he was taut and powerful, his wide shoulders squared in a vaguely threatening stance. He wore army fatigues, stained and torn, the shirt open at his throat and chest. His wind-tossed hair gleamed black as the October night and curled down onto his neck, much longer than she'd ever seen it. His smoke gray eyes glittered with a dangerous allure in the harsh, unshaven planes of his face.

He looked wild. Driven. As if he'd spent months on a desperate mission. Relief welled up in Elissa with such ferocity, it choked her. He hadn't gone. She hadn't lost him yet. Her breath caught on a sob. "I was afraid I'd never see you again."

"I'm not going anywhere." His gaze said much more.

She was in his arms, then, and something like lightning bolted through them. There was a blinding rush of sensation too intense to endure; a hellish force bent on parting them. His muscles strained to keep her against him, his arms were protective bars around her as he waged battle.

Elissa, too, fought the preternatural force with all her strength. She wanted so to hold him, to hold *on* to him, for as long as possible. She wanted to feel his breath against her cheek, his muscles beneath her fingers, his heartbeat against her own. That desire doubled as it forged with his.

"Elissa, I want you so much," he breathed against her ear.

She shut her eyes and inhaled his lusty male scent. He brushed his mouth along her jaw, then trailed hot, moist kisses down the side of her throat.

She dug her fingers into the hard muscles of his shoulders, relishing the sheer, primal joy his body gave her. He exhaled in a heated rush and from the base of her throat he dragged his tongue to the underside of her chin.

A response like thunder shook her to the core.

She met him in an openmouthed kiss that tasted of danger and freedom and a dark sweetness that was all his own. She matched him, thrust for thrust, swirl for swirl, drawing him in ever deeper. His large, rough hands slipped beneath her towel—caressing, rubbing, teasing her in ways that left both of them trembling with need.

He tugged her towel away and slung it down.

And then he stared. The pebbled tips of her breasts and the palms of his hands were wet and glistening. Mother's milk. Her cheeks flamed as she realized what it was. She moved to shield herself. He caught her arms and held them at her sides, his surprise turning to awe.

Bending her backward slightly, he lowered his mouth to her breast. With consummate reverence, he savored first one breast, then the other until she ached for him in a way she'd never ached before.

Her fingers found the rock-hard column behind his zipper and he growled under his breath. With tightly leashed passion, he reclaimed her mouth.

One kiss led to another. Deeper, hotter, wilder. His

hand skimmed down the curve of her hip to the velvet of her inner thighs. Then, ever so slowly, it traveled upward, to her most intimate valley.

Elissa inhaled sharply at his unexpected touch.

His fingers lightly played there. His tongue danced in her mouth. Pleasure flashed through her in waves, bringing her blood to a full simmer.

Whimpering deep in her throat, awash in relentless sensation, she clung to him. She pushed against him writhing, her hip brushing against his hardness. He groaned, clutched her tighter and broke out in a sweat.

His ministrations slowed. Then intensified.

She dragged her mouth away from his to cry out, but suddenly his fingers ceased their taunting and came to rest, feather-light, against the threshold she so wished him to enter.

Poignant anticipation held her virtually paralyzed. Her mouth opened wide in a silent gasp. Her eyes sought his.

Slowly, obligingly, he deepened the touch.

Pleasure blossomed within her to an unbearable force.

His gaze, hooded with passion, burned into her like molten silver. In a hoarse, almost pained plea, he asked, "Will you let me love you, Elissa?"

Unable to summon her voice—or even to nod, for fear she'd shatter to pieces, Elissa merely gazed at him with all her heart. He had asked her permission the first time they'd made love, too. He had forced her to say it out loud. His need to do so suffused her with a profound emotion. Hadn't he known she was his for the taking?

If he hadn't, he did now.

He read it in her eyes.

Jesse lifted her off the floor, onto the bed. Elation blazed through him, along with the fiercest desire. If she had refused him, he surely would have died. For the heat had consumed him entirely, with much more devastation than it had even in his fantasies.

He needed her now, in the worst way. Needed to taste her again. To trace with his mouth the seductive path his hands had forged. To bring her to the brink of delirium, then pull her back, until she begged him with her eyes and her whispers and her body. To plunge himself into her again and again until her very soul merged with his.

AT HER SON'S HUNGRY WAIL, Elissa opened her eyes and stretched with languid contentment against the hard male body behind her. She'd been possessed last night—every intimate part of her—with a thoroughness she had never imagined, by the only man who had ever incited her to passion.

Her muscles ached with a delicious soreness, and as the memory of their lovemaking returned in full, her blood fairly sang with feminine power. For she had possessed *him* last night, too, as fully as a woman could possess a man.

If she were a violin, she thought with a smug smile, her strings would still be humming.

As she thought of the bow that had played her with such exquisite artistry, her hand appreciatively caressed the furry, muscular arm wrapped around her midsection. If only the baby wouldn't holler so; she'd love to spend a few more hours snuggled in these powerful arms.

But Cody demanded his breakfast, and she couldn't allow him to remain hungry for even a second longer than necessary. Reluctantly, she lifted the arm that lay heavily across her waist. But as she sat up to slip out from under it, a shock of cold horror pulsated through her.

*She couldn't see the arm.* She could feel it in detail: smooth, muscle-corded, hairy. But she couldn't see it!

Her heart stood still for a petrified moment. Chill bumps rose on every inch of her still-naked body. Winding her fists in the bedsheet that was tangled around her waist, she peered over her shoulder toward the masculine being who breathed rhythmically beside her.

*No one lay there.*

Her scalp prickled, as if her hair stood on end. Blood rushed to her head in a dizzying *whoosh.* And with a panicked cry, she scrambled from the bed, lunging and falling across the room, yanking the tangled bedsheet with her.

Behind her she heard a surprised mutter, a vivid curse, and the violent *thump* of a large body hitting the floor on the other side of the bed.

"Jesse!" she cried, quivering where she stood, clinging to the bedsheet as if to shield herself from further horror. "What's happened to you?"

Another descriptive curse, and then he said, "What the hell do you *think* happened? You pulled the sheet out from under me. Rolled me out of the damned bed!"

"But you...you...I can't...I can't..."

"*You* can't?" The utterance sounded weak, almost dazed, and still came from the floor, as if he hadn't fully risen. "Hell, I feel like a goddamn tank's run over me." After a pause, he noted in an almost pained whisper, "Baby's crying."

"Jesse!" Concern washed away a good deal of her

horror. She sprang out of her stupor and shrugged into her bathrobe. "Are you okay?"

"Can't say I am." It was little more than a hoarse rasping. With a weak attempt at wryness, he croaked, "Not enough lovin'."

Worry now gnawed at her, and she dashed around the bed, hoping to see him lying there in full living color. But when she reached the far side where he had fallen, she halted in dismay.

She saw not a sign of him anywhere. "I can't see you," she burst out in an agonized whisper. "You're inv-visible." She thought she heard a dry expletive, but with Cody's howling, she couldn't be sure. "Is this because...because we...made love?" she cried, wishing she could see him.

In reply came a strangled "Hell, no."

She edged toward the head of the bed, feeling carefully along the floor with her bare feet. Surely she'd feel him sitting or lying here, maybe nursing a morning headache....

"Jesse, where are you?" She knelt near the head of the bed, groping the air in all directions as if she might have missed him in the narrow space between the bed and the wall.

But she felt nothing. No warm male body. Not even a mysterious cold spot. Jesse, it seemed, had left her again.

At least, she supposed he had.

"Dr. Lehmberg? Elissa Sinclair." She was sitting with her knees against her chest on the Persian carpet in Jesse's living room, her back against the sofa and the telephone receiver to her ear. As she spoke, she absently watched Cody play with Mr. Duckie on the blanket she'd laid out for him. "I have another question."

"Sure," encouraged the professor. "What is it?"

"What would happen to a ghost if he—" she hesitated a moment, then forced the words out "—if he made love? With a live human being, I mean."

Silence echoed loudly over the telephone line. She could visualize her former teacher's surprise as the seconds ticked by. "What do you mean, made love?"

"Oh, you know. The usual." Elissa cleared her throat and rubbed the back of her neck, which had grown uncomfortably warm. "Would it...*hurt*...the spirit? Weaken his life force somehow?"

"Are you saying that you know of a spirit that made love with someone?" Lehmberg's voice had undergone a subtle change—to one Elissa might have used as a counselor.

"Well, no, of course not." She already regretted her question. "Not personally, I mean."

"Then what did you mean?"

She couldn't think of a single lie.

"Elissa, have you seen the apparition again that we discussed in my office?"

"Yes," she admitted, clutching the receiver tighter.

"Does it take the shape of a...man?"

"Uh-huh."

"You're not crying, are you?"

"Not quite," she warbled, holding back tears.

"Oh, Elissa, calm down. I've already told you how strong-minded spirits can create multisensory illusions that could be quite convincing to the average person."

"This wasn't an illusion. It couldn't have been. I felt it, he was here, k-kissing me, and..." She stopped and dashed a tear from her cheek. "It was real, I swear."

"This man—did you know him when he was alive?"

Sensing a trap, she replied cautiously, "Somewhat."

"Somewhat? So he wasn't a loved one?"

The simple question hit her with surprising force. Was Jesse a "loved one"? In that moment, a profound realization swept through her.

"Yes," she whispered. "He is." And it was true. She loved Jesse—in a way she'd loved no other man. She had from the moment she'd met him. "He's the father of my child."

A sigh, or something suspiciously like it, sounded in the receiver. "You should have told me that to begin with."

"Does it make a difference?"

"Not technically speaking. But—" Lehmberg paused, as if trying to pick her next words carefully. "I'm not saying that you haven't experienced a spiritual visitation. But often when a person sees the ghost of a loved one for any longer than a brief appearance, it has more to do with grief than with anything paranormal."

Elissa stiffened, her disappointment strong. "You think I'm imagining all this?"

"I didn't say that, exactly. But sometimes a person's psyche can conjure up whatever he or she most desires."

"You, a scientist in the field of parapsychology, think I'm just hallucinating? You think I dreamed up Jesse for company, or maybe a hot date on a lonely night?"

"I wouldn't put it in those words, but—"

"I know what grief is, Dr. Lehmberg, and I know the difference between wishful thinking and fact. Sure, I wish he hadn't died. Sure, I wish we could have had a future together." Her voice broke, but she kept on, her indignation painful. "That doesn't mean I've flipped my lid and now go around making love to illusions."

"Pity. That might have its advantages. Less worry about sexually transmitted diseases."

It took a stunned moment for Elissa to realize that Lehmberg was joking. The muted humor helped her regain perspective in a way nothing else would have. The professor wouldn't joke with a person she suspected might be crazy, would she? With a mollified sniff, Elissa mumbled, "Saves money on contraceptives, too."

That provoked a brief laugh. Elissa felt relieved, as if their relationship had been somewhat restored. "The Elissa Sinclair I know," said Lehmberg, the sobriety back in her voice, "would be the first to doubt any phenomena that couldn't be fully explained."

"That's right."

"Which is why you have to consider all possibilities. If this apparition truly is from the spiritual realm, the first thing you have to do is convince him that he's dead."

"I tried. He wouldn't believe me."

"That's not unusual. Ask any psychic who's worked with earthbound spirits, and they'll tell you. The spirit usually doesn't realize he's dead. It's up to you, Elissa, to convince him otherwise. Then you may have to guide him."

"Guide him? Where?"

"To the other side. Think of him as a traveler who has lost his way. He needs to be directed toward the light."

"What light?"

"Haven't you read accounts of near-death experiences? Documented cases date way back into history, and almost all of them share a common element: the departing soul is beckoned toward a brilliant light, usually at the end of a tunnel. If you really want to help this spirit, Elissa, you'll have to make him understand that he must leave this mortal plane and move on toward the light."

Dismay curled through her. She didn't want to imagine Jesse walking through that tunnel. "But maybe he's not ready. Maybe he hasn't achieved his final goal."

"If that's the case, he probably won't go," she replied with characteristic aplomb. "But he'll find no peace, no happiness, until he does. Who knows what damage he'll suffer, the longer he's kept from his destiny?" Somberly she added, "Perhaps he'll simply cease to exist."

Elissa swallowed a sudden lump in her throat; a painful heaviness pushed against her chest. "What if he doesn't reappear to me?"

"That would probably mean he found his way on his own."

Her vision slowly blurred, and she foolishly nodded above the receiver, not trusting her voice enough to reply.

"It's odd," murmured Lehmberg, "the degree of communication you seem to have established with the departed. Are you, by any chance, psychic?"

"Me? No. I mean, I never thought of myself as psychic." After a reflective moment, she mused, "But my mother did often accuse me of reading her mind. And a few times, I knew when a friend was about to pay an unexpected visit. I just felt it, somehow."

"So you've always had some psychic tendencies."

Elissa shrugged. "I suppose."

"That might account for the degree of communication you've established. You know, Elissa," she said as if pondering a new idea, "I've read theories that a truly psychic individual could actually summon the dead."

"Summon—? You mean, *I* might have held Jesse back from his final destiny?"

"It's just a theory. Other parapsychologists dismiss it as a bunch of nonsense. I tend to agree with the latter. I feel that only the individual himself could make the choice of whether or not to follow that beckoning light."

Elissa shut her eyes, more confused than ever. "But maybe my...my wanting him...is keeping him here longer than he would have otherwise stayed."

"Maybe. Anyway, try what I've told you. Guide him toward the light." Professor Lehmberg then wished her luck and murmured a pleasant goodbye.

But before she broke their connection, she imparted one last bit of advice. "It wouldn't hurt for you to talk to a grief counselor. The entire problem may be an emotional one. Sometimes when it comes to love, it's just too hard to let go. That unresolved business might actually be your own."

Elissa hung up the phone with an even greater ache splitting her heart. She had to send Jesse away, toward his final destiny. And she couldn't allow her own feelings to hold him back.

If only she didn't love him so.

SHE SPENT THE REST of that Saturday morning pacing around the house and yard with Cody in her arms, on constant guard for sound and movement. Inside, she jumped at shadows and settling noises of the old house; outside, at every whisper of wind or crackle of leaves.

Could Jesse still be with her, but unable to appear, or to speak? The horror she'd felt that morning at finding him invisible returned with almost as much force.

"Jesse," she found herself saying out loud, "are you here? Can you hear me, can you see me?"

If so, he wasn't saying.

It didn't stop her from talking to him, though, all that day and night. As she lit a cozy evening fire in the hearth, she asked if he was sharing it with her. As she climbed the staircase, she asked if he was following. And as she undressed for her bath and soaked in the jasmine-scented water, she gazed around and asked if he was watching.

She wished he were.

She dressed for bed with slow, deliberately seductive moves, in the soft, pearl-white gown she hadn't yet worn for him. She sat at the mirror of an antique vanity and brushed her hair, watching for movement behind her. She even sprayed her wrists and breasts lightly with perfume, all in an attempt to lure him out into the open.

But Jesse failed to put in an appearance.

Proof, she thought. He positively wasn't here.

The following morning, a cloudy Sunday, she dressed Cody in the little yellow sweater and cap she had knitted for him and pushed him in his stroller down the driveway, across the narrow road, to the sharply sloping bluff above the Skidaway River. Tall grasses rippled in the autumn breeze down the slope to the hazel green water. Long, wooden planked walkways above the marsh grass led to boathouses along the river bluff. Seabirds from the nearby Atlantic Ocean swooped and cried from the gray-and-white patchwork sky, their calls echoing her oppressive loneliness.

"I can't take much more of this, Jesse," she said, more from habit now than hope of eliciting a response. She stared out at a shrimp boat gliding past, its mast pole and cables glinting in the morning sun. "I can't stand not knowing where you are, or how you are, or if you'll come back."

"You think *I* like it?"

She jumped violently at the deep, quiet reply from beside her. He stood with his hands in the pockets of his gray trousers, a blue-green polo shirt emphasizing the incredible breadth of his chest. His jet hair rippled in the breeze like the marsh grass before them as he gazed solemnly across the river. "I don't like it worth a damn, not knowing when or where I'll black out, or come to."

It took Elissa a long moment to regain her breath from the shock of his appearance. "Don't do that!" she cried, a hand to her heart. "You scared me half to death!"

"We'd be there together, then, wouldn't we?"

She stared at him, surprised that he'd say such a thing. "Well, yes, I suppose 'half to death' would pretty much describe where you are." Her heart gradually stopped galloping and her voice returned to a civilized pitch. "So, you believe me now? That you're...dead?"

"Of course not. I was humoring you." He flashed her a mischievous grin, then bent down to gaze eye level at Cody in the stroller. The baby was totally occupied with stuffing all ten of his chubby little fingers into his mouth. "Come here to your pa," Jesse mumbled. And he reached to take the bright-eyed baby from the stroller.

"No, don't touch him."

He stopped with his hands inches from Cody and plied Elissa with a dark, questioning frown.

"People might see and wonder how he's hovering in midair. Besides, you shouldn't touch anyone. I'm afraid you'll disappear. Maybe this time for good."

Jesse settled his hands on his hips and stared at her. As much as he wanted to argue, he knew she was at least partially right. Something about physical contact with other people did put a drain on his energy. And he didn't want to fade off into unconsciousness again. Yet neither could he abide the idea of not touching Cody or her. No, that wouldn't do at all.

He made another move for Cody, and Elissa pulled the stroller back from him. "Aren't you worried about yourself? You saw the reaction of the people in town. They couldn't see you! And where did you go after that? It's not exactly normal to be bothered by pesky disappearing spells."

"Of course I'm concerned," he replied. But not as much as he knew he should be. In fact, nothing seemed too terribly important—his health, his mysterious ailment, even the military screwup about his alleged death. The only thing that mattered, he realized, was making Elissa want him with the same urgency he wanted her.

He stared out at the river, stunned by the depth of his need for her. He'd always been the one to hightail it out of a relationship at the first sign of intimacy. Now he found himself craving it, like some addictive drug. He was hooked, irrevocably hooked, and he meant for her to be just as needful of him.

His pondering was interrupted by the soft, throaty voice that had haunted his dreams, both sleeping and waking, for a full dozen months. "Does it hurt you, Jesse? Disappearing?"

"Yes." He turned his gaze fully on her. "It hurt like hell to leave your bed."

Her sherry brown eyes warmed beneath his stare, reflecting the intimacy of their lovemaking. She broke their gaze, a delicate flush rising on her cheeks. "That's not what I meant. You're deliberately avoiding the issue."

"I'd say you're avoiding it." His eyes spoke with a seriousness that raised her temperature. "Let's go inside and build a fire in the hearth. Then you can take a bath with that oil that glistens all over your skin." His glance took in all of her, as if he was envisioning it. "Then after we dry you off, I'll help you brush your hair."

She cast him a wondering glance. His plan sounded very much like her activities of last night.

"And maybe you can find some fancy gown." His voice had grown husky. "You know, like the ones with those thin little straps and see-through lace, clear down past here." He swept his finger from her shoulder to the tip of her breast, not actually touching her, but gliding above her thin sweater with an aura that sizzled right through it.

"Jesse, stop!" Ridiculously aroused, she crossed her arms and glanced around. "Someone might be watching."

"I thought you said they can't see me."

"Probably not, but—"

"So I can do anything I want...and no one would see."

She recognized the teasing light in his eyes—and the sensuality that sizzled beneath it. "Were you there," she whispered, "in my bedroom last night?"

"I dreamed I was there. I dreamed you wore a sexy white gown, with your hair all shiny and loose around your shoulders. And you sprayed perfume between your breasts. It smelled sweet—like oranges and powdered sugar. I wanted to taste it on you."

Her breath caught. "I wore a gown like you described. And sprayed perfume that smells very much like..."

"Did you whisper to me?" he interrupted hoarsely.

She nodded. And they slipped into a gaze, deep and warm with mutual longing. As his lips neared her, she abruptly came to her sense. "Jesse, *we can't touch.*"

"The hell we can't." And he reached for her.

She had anticipated the move and drew away. "I'm afraid you'll disappear!"

"That's just something I'll have to learn to control. I can use the practice."

"Practice!" Resolutely, she locked gazes with him, somber and earnest this time. "Listen to me, Jesse, and believe every word that I say. This might be a hard concept to grasp, but it's important that you do. *You are dead.*"

He nodded, slipped his hands into his pockets and tried not to curse. Her confounded "dead" theory was definitely cramping his style. "I understand why you think that. This invisibility thing...well, it *is* hard to explain."

"What other explanation is there?"

"Could be the result of a military experiment." But in his heart, he knew better. Whatever was happening to him went much deeper than his body, or even his mind. He knew that now with a clarity beyond reason. He also knew he couldn't give in to it, whatever it was. He had to overcome it.

"If some technology turned you invisible," reasoned Elissa, "then why can *I* see you?"

He shrugged, at a loss for an answer. "If I am, as you say, dead...why can you see me?"

"Because you're haunting me."

"Haunting you!" He frowned at her, incensed. "What, like some paranormal stalker?"

"When we talked, you said you couldn't remember anything from the times we're apart. Your spells of consciousness all take place while you're with me. Is that still true?"

"Well, yes, but—"

"That's because *you're haunting me*. If a ghost is haunting a house, he stays with it. He doesn't take a night off to paint the town. Face it, Jesse—you're haunting me."

"Now, why would I do a thing like that?"

"I'm not sure." She averted her eyes, looking somewhat secretive, as if she knew full well why he'd do it, but preferred not to say. "My research says," she began slowly, "that ghosts often remain earthbound because of their desire to fulfill some unachieved goal or obligation."

"What goal have I left unachieved?"

She pressed her lips together, obviously reluctant to answer. Just when he thought she wouldn't, she said, "At first, I thought you wanted to see Cody, and to hold him. But you've already done that and you're still here."

"Yes, I am. At least we agree on something."

"Maybe your unresolved business has something to do with guilt."

"Guilt?" he repeated in surprise. "About what?"

"Failing to contact me when I informed you of my pregnancy. And when Cody was born." Though her voice remained level, he could hear her resentment. "It wasn't until your deathbed, Jesse, that you regretted your neglect."

"Neglect! I didn't neglect Cody or you."

"Death endowed you with a conscience. Apparently you now feel the need to atone."

A muscle in his jaw throbbed. "Damn it, Elissa, I told you I was on a highly sensitive, covert mission. My mail was held until I returned to the base—"

"I know. The colonel backed up your story. Your mission clearly accounts for the last few months of my pregnancy. But what about the first half dozen? He refused to say when your mission started, or how long it lasted."

"Of course he refused to say. That's classified information. But I swear, I didn't receive your letters until I returned from my mission, two days before my flight home. The minute I knew of his existence, I legally acknowledged Cody as my son. Furthermore, I couldn't have 'regretted my neglect' on my deathbed because I haven't *been* on my deathbed yet!"

She would have believed him about the letters, about his immediate interest in Cody, except for what Dean had told her about the calls from brothels in Asia. Dean had begged him to at least talk to her about the pregnancy, but Jesse had refused. *Just because I play a game of pool,* he'd said, *doesn't mean I want to lug the pool table around with me.*

Thinking about those conversations that Dean had reluctantly relayed to her brought back all the hurt and humiliation she had suffered. She wanted to fling those heartless comments in Jesse's face, just to watch his new postmortem conscience kick him in the butt.

But wasn't his conscience kicking him hard enough already? Hard enough to keep him from his ever-after!

Besides, she had promised Dean that she'd never use the things he told her to drive a wedge between his cousin and him.

"Just forget I said anything about guilt," she grumbled, ashamed of herself for almost betraying Dean's confidence.

"You don't believe me, do you." Jesse's dark gaze bore into her with patent incredulity. "You really think I read those letters and chose to ignore them."

Goaded by his act of persecuted innocence, she retorted, "Mail isn't the only method of modern communication."

"What do you mean by that? Did you try to call me? If so, I never got the message, not even after I returned to the base. Tell me who you spoke with, and we'll confront them together."

My, but he was convincing! She rounded on him in barely leashed fury, "You can't confront anyone. You're dead!"

His jaw clenched, his stare simmered, but he answered with impressive restraint, "I am not dead. And whether you believe me or not, the only unresolved business I have is to be there for Cody, as his father, while he grows up."

A bright flash of pain sliced through Elissa's anger. She wished it could be so. She wished it with all her heart. But a future of any kind was impossible for Jesse.

Her thwarted longing made the memory of his past betrayal hurt all the more. "Yes, I suppose that does make sense," she reflected with quiet anguish. "That would be a way for you to atone for your initial neglect, whether you ever admit to your guilt or not." To her horror, she felt her eyes blur with tears. "Sorry to tell you, though—you're one lifetime too late!"

He muttered a curse and grabbed her, his hands hard and forceful on her upper arms. "I intended from the first moment I knew about him to be a father to Cody. Trust me on this, Elissa. Trust me."

The familiar electricity flashed through them at his touch, but he didn't fight it this time. He wanted to saturate her with his emotions.

She felt his righteous anger, his determination to be believed, and above all, his burning need. The force of it was too powerful to endure and pried them apart, propelling her from his grasp.

Shaken to the core, Elissa caught her balance against a tree, too dizzy to see straight, too confused to make sense of things. She'd felt no guilt from him. No deception. He truly seemed to believe what he was telling her.

But how could that be? Dean surely hadn't lied, especially not when he'd known how dire her situation was.

"Trust me, Elissa" came Jesse's ragged whisper.

She released her supporting hold on the tree trunk and looked around for him, but he was nowhere to be seen.

"Jesse!" she cried. "Don't you dare leave me now!"

She received no answer. Disappointment, frustration and self-blame violently assaulted her. Why had she goaded him into a quarrel? Why had she allowed him to touch her? She hadn't even tried to guide him toward the beckoning light. She hadn't had a chance to forgive him...regardless of what he had or had not done in the wretched past.

Heartsick for wasting what might have been her last encounter with him, Elissa weakly returned to where Cody sucked his fingers and watched her from his stroller.

A fog had begun to descend in wispy swirls above

the river. The black Spanish moss on the branches of the towering oaks swayed ghostlike. A seagull dove from a low-hanging cloud, his cry sharp and mocking.

Elissa blindly stared into the thickening mist, her throat aching with wasted chances. "I'm not finished talking to you yet, Jesse!" she admonished out loud, grasping the stroller bar until her fingers hurt.

Though he hadn't quite enough energy left to voice a reply, Jesse thought, *I'm not finished with you yet, either.*

A car motored past Elissa on the narrow road, then pulled into Jesse's driveway. A dusty tan station wagon. The look of surprise on her face told Jesse she hadn't been expecting visitors.

The car door opened and a familiar stodgy form with sandy brown curls and wire-rimmed glasses unfolded from the driver's seat.

Dean. With a small bouquet of roses in one hand and an overnight bag in the other.

# 9

"DEAN, WHAT ARE YOU doing here?"

Elissa's wide-eyed greeting gave Jesse no clue as to whether she considered the surprise a pleasant one. He himself would have phrased the question differently. He would have said what the *hell* are you doing here.

Unfortunately, his brief contact with Elissa had siphoned his energy to a dangerous low. He tried to speak, but found he had no voice. And he was obviously invisible even to Elissa.

This handicap was getting more annoying by the moment.

From the grin on Dean's face as he shuffled toward Elissa, Jesse knew his cousin felt confident about the welcome he'd receive. "I was worried about you and Cody being here alone. And I missed you too much." He planted a kiss on her cheek. "So I spent yesterday working on plans for my sub, and arranged personal leave for tomorrow and Tuesday."

He handed her the bouquet of red roses with a courtly bow. It had been just that kind of cornball move that had earned Dean jeers throughout school—and had drawn Jesse into fistfights to vindicate him.

As Elissa murmured her thanks, Dean squatted down beside the stroller. "And how's our little man?" He pulled from his sweater pocket a yellow, pretzel-shaped teething ring that squeaked as he squeezed it.

Cody reached for it with a smile, his chubby legs kicking beneath the stroller tray.

A vague ache twisted through Jesse. His son responded immediately to Dean, but hadn't even seen Jesse. Brusquely, he told himself he should be glad that Cody liked Dean. He was, after all, his cousin. Probably the closest Cody would ever have to an uncle. *And maybe the closest he'll have to a father.* Jesse scowled at the thought. *He* was Cody's father, and always would be.

Why, then, did Dean's presence fill him with resentment? Dean had been like a younger brother to him all through their boyhood—irritating at times with his holier-than-thou attitude, but always an ally at home where the adults stood united in chronic disapproval of Jesse.

Dean and he had fished together near the family's beach cottage on Tybee Island, and they'd water-skied. Or rather, Jesse had skied while Dean drove the boat and muttered dire predictions about the shark-infested waters. Jesse had shown him his first girlie magazine, back when that was high excitement. They'd been like brothers.

The night before Jesse was to ship out for his overseas mission, the premonition of death had been riding heavy in his gut. He had stopped to say goodbye to Dean; an impulsive visit, but one that had seemed important.

The visit *had* proven important, but for a different reason than he'd expected. That night he'd met and made love to Elissa.

It was only now, as he watched Dean play up to her, that his resentment kicked in. Dean ruffled the baby's dark, wispy hair, then rose from his squatting position. Reaching into the pocket of his cardigan, he brought out a rectangular box and handed it to Elissa. "And this is for you."

Hesitantly, she opened it and eyed the contents in surprise. "A telephone."

"Cellular. I couldn't sleep a wink after you told me about that flat tire you had on the way here. Thank heavens you were able to change it."

Her cheeks pinkened and she avoided Dean's gaze. So, she hadn't told Dean about his presence. Her words from Friday morning returned to Jesse with new importance: *Everyone thinks you're dead. I think you're dead.* Did she plan to carry on as if he weren't there?

"This is sweet of you, Dean, but I can't accept—"

"I've already paid for the first month of basic service. Keep it at least until you're back home, safe and sound."

Jesse's lips stretched taut. As always, Dean had done the right thing. She *did* need a cellular phone while she was on the road. He himself should have thought of it.

With a sudden flash of insight, he recognized the look in Dean's besotted blue eyes as Elissa thanked him. It had been there when Dean had nursed obsessive crushes on girls at school. He hadn't acted on any of those crushes, way back then. He'd slept with their photos beneath his pillow, phoned them to hear their voices before he hung up, scrawled their names in his notebooks a thousand times over.

Jesse had been very careful to keep his hands off any woman Dean wanted. Dismay lodged like a rock in his stomach. Elissa would have to be the exception.

He watched as she scooped up Cody. Dean folded the stroller, packed it into her car and retrieved from his trunk two bags of groceries, which, he said, included fresh apples from a fruit stand, since he knew she loved them.

Jesse realized that he himself hadn't a clue as to what Elissa loved. Food-wise, at least. Then again, he knew exactly how to please her in other ways. Important ways. Ways that whetted a very different appetite.

Did Dean?

With teeth on edge, Jesse followed the couple as they climbed the front steps and entered his house. The oak door swung closed behind them and he put out a hand to stop it. The door didn't even slow as it shut in his face.

Jesse drew back and stared at his hand. *The door had passed right through it.* He tried to turn the knob, but his hand wouldn't connect with the solid material.

For the first time since he'd become aware of his "condition," alarm buzzed through him. He had passed through this door before, but only because he had wanted to, not because he couldn't open it.

With a technique he had deployed during the worst of his military endeavors, he cleared his mind of the alarm. He couldn't waste energy on unnecessary emotion. When his inner calm had been restored, he passed through the heavy oak door with only the slightest depletion of precious energy.

Once inside, he tried to lift an ashtray.

He couldn't, and the attempt left him weaker still. He had to rest, to marshal his strength, to stay silently on the sidelines. Until he could do more, of course. In a way he didn't fully understand, he retreated to an altered state that required the least amount of effort.

Throughout that Sunday afternoon, he observed their actions and heard the murmur of their conversation, but from an oddly distanced perspective. As if he were dreaming it.

Elissa took Dean on a tour of the house, then walked him around the gardens. They strolled down to the river, arm in arm, with Cody snuggled against Dean's shoulder. It wasn't until that evening, after they'd put Cody to bed and shared a supper of pot roast and vegetables, that Jesse's faculties sharpened. Elissa washed the dishes and Dean dried. They handed each other plates and glasses with smooth regularity, as if they'd been doing this kind of teamwork for years.

Cozy. Too damn cozy.

It hit Jesse then like a radar-guided missile: if he never returned to normal, if this affliction remained or grew worse, Dean would be a good husband for Elissa. A good father to Cody. He wondered if Elissa was in love with him.

Bleakness, gray and suffocating, descended on Jesse. She was a vibrant young woman, alone with a child. Why shouldn't she have fallen in love with a man who was always there for her?

A sick heaviness crowded his chest. He couldn't stand to think of her in Dean's arms. In Dean's bed. In Dean's life, as his woman, as his wife.

No, he couldn't accept that. Elissa was his. He didn't question the truth of this any more than he questioned his own existence. How could she not be meant for him? She filled up the emptiness that had once comprised the greater part of his soul. She'd replaced that emptiness with substance, warmth, vigor and light. No other man would claim her. Not if he could help it. But that's where the problem came in.

If this peculiar ailment continued, he'd be little more

than a fly on the wall. Maybe he was being selfish to want her for himself.

Shaken, Jesse tuned in to their conversation, determined to hear every word. He realized they were speaking about him.

"I'll miss him," Dean was saying as he dried a bowl. "Oh, I know we didn't have much in common. But we...we looked out for each other, Jesse and I."

Guilt weighted Jesse down. Here he was, fully intending to take Elissa away from Dean, while Dean stood mourning him.

"Not that Jesse was ever an angel." Dean shook his head at some amusing memory. "I could tell you some kind of stories."

Elissa lifted a brow, her interest caught. "Oh?"

Mild displeasure shaded Dean's eyes, as if he hadn't expected, or wanted, too much response to his melancholy musing. "Nothing you'd want to hear, actually."

"No, but I would. He *was* Cody's father," she reminded him. "I'd like to know as much as I can about him, to someday share with Cody."

His thin bottom lip drew so tight it almost disappeared. "You might not want to share Jesse's antics with an impressionable child."

Jesse raised his brows. Which stories had Dean planned to tell? As he thought back, though, he couldn't think of many he'd want Cody to imitate.

"Jesse couldn't have been all that bad," countered Elissa, "or he would have ended up in jail."

"He barely missed it. If it hadn't been for the family's influence..."

"Are you talking about the girls' dormitory incident?"

"That, and others. He started on the wrong road

early. While I was at my Scout meetings, he was loitering with a gang at the corner store, shoplifting."

It was true, Jesse had to admit. The thrill of danger had appealed to him even then.

"He stole his first car when he was thirteen," Dean went on. "Hot-wired the principal's Cadillac in the school lot."

Yep, Jesse remembered. He'd parked it three miles down the road. His popularity with the wild crowd had soared. He'd wondered at the time if it was his "bad blood" that made him crave the notoriety these pranks earned him.

"His *first* car?" said Elissa, looking clearly dismayed.

For the first time since it had happened, Jesse felt a stab of regret for the crime.

"He stole others, too?"

One, thought Jesse. Just one. Another prank.

"Oh, yes. Jesse was quite good at hot-wiring cars."

Jesse frowned. Dean made it sound as if he'd made a career out of stealing cars, but then, Dean's worst infraction had been turning in a poetry project late. Jesse must have seemed pretty hard core.

"He needed more guidance," pronounced Elissa, handing Dean another sudsy salad bowl.

"Guidance? Hah! He needed a lot more than guidance."

At Dean's resentful tone, Jesse narrowed his eyes on his cousin's face. Something was wrong here. He'd never heard or even imagined Dean talking about him with such hostility.

Yet, if Dean had been in love with Elissa, which he plainly was now, he couldn't have liked the fact that Jesse had slept with her. And fathered her child.

How stupid not to have seen it earlier! He hadn't realized Dean's feelings for Elissa until now.

Why hadn't Dean staked his claim to her that very first night they'd met? Why hadn't he at least mentioned how he felt about her before Jesse left the party with her? But Jesse already knew the answer to that. Because he had wanted her so damned badly, even then, and he'd made no bones about that fact. A head-on confrontation—especially with Jesse—had never been Dean's style.

"He wasn't only a juvenile delinquent," said Dean, sneering, "he was a bully and a heartbreaker, even in high school. He terrorized the boys—the good, decent ones—and used the girls for sex...the most vulnerable girls."

Poking her tongue against her cheek, Elissa scrubbed a skillet with unnecessary force. She wished she hadn't encouraged Dean to reminisce. He'd hit her where it hurt the most...in an old but not quite healed wound. Had Jesse pursued her that last night of his leave simply because he'd sensed she was vulnerable?

A sudden chill crept into the kitchen—an odd, unnatural cold. She glanced around, searching the shadows. She saw no trace of Jesse. Unnerved by the idea of him listening to their conversation—and by the hurtful conversation itself—she murmured, "It's not uncommon for high school boys to date a lot of girls."

"Yes, but—"

"I think I've heard enough about Jesse."

Silenced by her curt interruption, Dean gaped at her.

From beside her, Jesse's deep voice rushed against her ear, "Thanks for the defense, counselor. Took you long enough to shut him up."

Elissa dropped her dishcloth and sloshed water over

the sink basin. Grasping the counter to steady herself, she turned to find no one beside her. Or rather, no one visible.

She glanced back to Dean and realized he hadn't heard Jesse. Dean stood watching her through his wire-rimmed glasses with concerned bewilderment. "I'm sorry if I offended you, Elissa. I never meant to." In a low murmur he added, "Perhaps it's best for you that Jesse's gone."

She wanted to shout that it wasn't. She wished desperately that Jesse were alive and permanently visible.

"Aren't you going to tell him I'm here?" asked the wry, disembodied voice of the man who was making her crazy.

"No!"

Dean broke off in the middle of a statement about his desire to see her with the roses back in her cheeks. "Pardon me?" he said, blinking.

"Nothing," she muttered. "I just...chipped a nail."

"Tell him to go," Jesse directed. "This is my house, and I don't want him here."

Elissa bit her tongue, afraid that she might be goaded into responding again. How would Dean react? He certainly wouldn't believe Jesse was here. He'd think she'd gone crazy. Unless, of course, Jesse started moving things around the room or slamming doors.

Anxiety hummed through her as she envisioned it. Knowing Dean, he'd call whatever authorities he felt should be notified. The so-called experts would then come to study Jesse. Some might try to exorcise him. The media would sensationalize him. Who knows what else would come of it?

One thing was certain—she would no longer have

the opportunity of staying alone with him. He'd belong to the curious. She would lose him.

"Excuse me, Dean, I'd better go check on Cody." She dried her hands, hurried from the kitchen and raced up the stairs.

She ducked into her bedroom, closed the door and turned to find Jesse standing there, solidly visible in a pair of close-fitting jeans and a dark sweater, his arms crossed and his smoke gray eyes impatient.

"You have to stop disappearing and appearing like that," she railed. "It's driving me crazy! How can I talk to Dean when you're standing a few feet away from him, invisible?"

"I agree, it poses a problem. Send him away."

"If I asked him to leave now, he'd know something was wrong and then he'd refuse to leave. What would it hurt, letting him stay one night? After all, he *is* your cousin."

"I don't care if he's my long-lost twin." His gaze arrested hers with all the urgency he felt building inside him. Gruffly, he whispered, "I want to have you alone."

Warm color touched her cheeks. Her hand fluttered to the base of her neck, where he swore he could see her heartbeat. "But I can't send Dean away tonight." Despite her words, her voice had deepened to a honeyed richness.

Jesse loved the fact that he could affect her so. But on the heels of that gratifying thought came a tormenting one: *could Dean?*

"His feelings would be hurt if I asked him to leave." Her eyes were the luminous color of candlelit burgundy. "Besides, he's worried about me. It would be better to show him that Cody and I are perfectly all right here by ourselves so he'll go home satisfied."

"Judging by those roses, I think it'll take a little more than peace of mind to 'satisfy' him."

She stared blankly at him for a moment, then slowly lowered her jaw. "Are you insinuating he brought me those roses just to—to—" She spluttered into speechlessness, then burst out, "How dare you cheapen his kindness that way! Just because *you* can't think past your zipper doesn't mean Dean can't."

Jesse wanted to grab her by the shoulders and shake some sense into her. Or maybe kiss the sense right out of her. But he couldn't touch her. He couldn't risk losing contact with her again. "Those roses mean one thing and one thing only. He can't wait to get his hands on you." *And then I'll have to kill him.*

Elissa stiffened and lifted her chin. "I've spent a lot of time with Dean in the past ten years, and he's always been kind, considerate, generous...."

"Are you telling me you haven't slept with him?"

She planted her fists on her hips and glowered. "I'm not telling you anything."

He stared at her hard and long, as if rifling through her thoughts to find an answer to his question. On a peculiarly jagged note, he finally queried, "Are you in love with him?"

She opened her mouth to tell him no, but stopped. How unfair to Dean to tell Jesse something so personal about their relationship before she explained it to Dean himself.

When she didn't answer, Jesse shut his eyes in a brief, hard wince. When he reopened them, they'd grown infinitely colder. His voice emerged as smooth and polished as a sea-washed stone. "Has he worked up enough courage yet to pop the big question?"

"He *has* asked me to marry him, if that's what you mean."

Though Jesse hadn't been moving much to begin with, he seemed to lapse into a concentrated state of immobility—as if breath itself had left his body. "And...?" he prompted.

"And what?"

"Do you plan to marry him?"

"That's none of your business."

Movement returned to him then in the form of a harsh scowl. "The hell it's not. The man you marry will live with my son, at least part of the time. You don't think I'd let you and Dean have full custody of Cody, do you?"

She retreated a step, her hand to her heart, her back to the solid oak door. "Jesse, you can't—"

"Don't be too sure about what I can or cannot do. If you marry Dean, I'll damn sure share custody of my son."

"And if I don't?" she asked faintly.

"Then, when I'm home on leave or stationed nearby, I'll keep Cody. You'd be welcome to stay with us, if you'd like. Or, to simplify matters—" his gaze intensified and his voice lowered to a rough whisper "—we can marry."

Elissa gaped at him, stunned. "You and I?"

"No, I thought we'd advertise for spouses in the personal ads. Of course, you and I."

"You'd do that, for...Cody?"

His lips tightened, his nostrils flared. "I don't see why not. I intended to change his name to Garrett, anyway."

Her bottom lip jutted out with sudden anger. "I'll marry whomever I damn well please, and I promise you this—it won't be you. I don't ask for much in a man, but I do prefer him alive!"

"Elissa?" Dean's voice intruded from the other side of the bedroom door, startling her. "Who are you talking to?"

"I'm...talking...on the phone," she improvised. "Why don't you go downstairs and make that popcorn you brought? It's almost time for your television shows."

"They've already started." He sounded petulant, just short of whiny. "I thought you'd be down there by now."

"I'll be down in a moment." She waited until his footsteps thudded down the stairs before she turned back to Jesse. "Dean doesn't deserve to be thrown out of your house like a sack of garbage. He's a good man. An honest man. A man who stood by me when *others* didn't."

Her emphasis on the word "others" furrowed Jesse's brow. "Do you mean me?"

"If the shoe fits..."

"That's the whole problem between us, isn't it, Elissa? You think I ignored your letters. I'm telling you one last time: I didn't even see them until I got back from my mission. For one thing, you used my old address. A *very* old address. I was lucky they even reached—" Jesse stopped. "Where did you get that address?"

She pursed her lips and stared, refusing to say.

"It was Dean, wasn't it." And the picture slid into clear focus. Disturbingly clear focus. Anger—and a dull sense of betrayal—flushed through him, washing away illusions built over a lifetime. As the initial surge of anger ebbed, Jesse realized another truth. He hadn't ever counted too heavily on Dean's support. He hadn't—

and didn't—believe too much in *anyone's* support of him.

He'd always known deep inside that he was alone.

"You're angry about Dean giving me your address," Elissa said. She crossed her arms and watched him with eyes that glittered accusingly. "He said you would be. Don't you dare hold it against him. I was pregnant with your child. To Dean, that was justification enough to break his promise."

"He told you I made him promise not to give you my address?" No wonder she'd been so peeved. Clever, Jesse had to admit. In one fell swoop, Dean had alienated Elissa from him *and* sabotaged their communication.

"Why didn't you want me to have your address, Jesse?" she probed, both anger and sadness in her voice. "What were you afraid I'd do with it?"

"I never told him to keep my address from you. In fact, I deliberately gave him my current one." He plied her with a searching gaze. "Why do you think he gave you an address that hasn't been good for more than eight years now?"

She blinked, taken aback, but after a moment, she shrugged. "He obviously thought that was your current address."

"He wrote the real one on the back of his hairstylist's business card and slipped it into his wallet."

*That* surprised her, though she refused to be swayed into doubting her knight in shining armor. "None of that matters now. If Dean has to leave this house tonight, so do I."

Anger tightened every muscle in Jesse's body. "Go ahead. But you won't take Cody. I'll make sure of that." A bluff, and he knew it. His energy level was too low now to do much of anything, or he would have already strangled Dean. In truth, he barely had enough energy to remain visible to Elissa. Fortunately, she wasn't aware of that. Another lesson he'd learned in the course of his military career—when low on weapons or men, *bluff.*

Elissa squared her jaw. "Don't threaten me, Jesse." With one last glare, she stalked out of the bedroom.

He knew then that he'd made a gross tactical error. Instead of making her see that Dean was the intruder, he had placed himself in that role. *He* was the enemy now, as far as she was concerned. She might even turn to Dean for help.

Jesse gritted his teeth. He'd been a damn fool, trying to keep her with him by force, virtually holding her baby hostage. What the hell kind of strategy was that? No better than a terrorist's.

He wanted his son, yes. And he wanted Elissa. But not under duress. He wanted her to know the truth about him and his reaction to her letters. He wanted her to stay with him of her own free will. He wanted her to want him.

How to make her believe his word against a man she'd known for ten years as a friend and maybe a lover? She'd known Jesse for days, not years, and in that brief time, he'd brought her only misery and shame.

He cursed the mission that had kept him out of touch with her, cursed his cousin for his sly deceit. Most of all, he cursed his own blind stupidity.

He clearly saw the enemy now.

Time for a forward advance. He had no weapons. He couldn't as much as lift an ashtray, let alone assert physical force. He couldn't be heard to issue challenges or ultimatums; he couldn't even be seen, except by Elissa.

Nevertheless, the battle line would have to be drawn. His cousin would have to defend his actions or pay the price for his sabotage. Elissa would have to choose *her* side of that battle line.

# 10

ELISSA RETURNED TO the living room, gritting her teeth. Jessie had gone too far this time, trying to pin the blame for his own neglect on Dean. If Dean had indeed given her the wrong address for Jesse, it must have been an innocent mistake.

Besides, even if her letter hadn't reached Jesse in time, Dean had spoken with him over the phone, not once, but many times before his mission began. According to Dean, Jesse hadn't wanted to speak *to* her or *about* her.

A sudden doubt permeated her anger. Was it fair to Jesse to withhold her knowledge of those calls? Should she have broken Dean's confidence and demanded that Jesse explain? He'd only deny making the calls. What else could he do?

But the niggling doubt persisted. Was Jesse a liar? *Was he?* She honestly didn't know. She wanted to believe he wasn't. But his own family had warned her repeatedly that he had ways of convincing women—especially vulnerable women—of anything. And with Jesse, she was indeed vulnerable.

He'd had the gall to ask her to marry him in order to "simplify" his visits with Cody. As if she had nothing better to do with her life than to make things convenient for him. The man's ego was nothing short of delusional.

And yet, for the briefest moment, she'd been tempted to accept his offer!

If that wasn't proof of onsetting insanity, what was?

Silently admonishing herself for allowing any man to demolish her better judgment, she settled back against the sofa cushions beside Dean. Absently, she toyed with the crossword puzzle in her lap—another of Dean's gifts, and part of a ritual they'd fallen into: television, popcorn and crossword puzzles. She stared in the direction of the television that had already mesmerized him into a stupor.

What, she wondered, would be Jesse's next step? The question made her nervous. She'd infuriated him, she knew. It was only a matter of time before he'd retaliate. Unless, of course, he faded out again.

Despite her irritation with him, worry spiraled through her. Surely he wouldn't fade away for good, just because she'd angered him?

*No*, she told herself, remembering the insults he'd just slung at her. He was too mean to vanish that easily. But he wouldn't hurt Cody or her, and she seriously doubted he'd hurt his own cousin. So whatever his next move might be, she'd simply ignore him.

She fiddled with her pencil above her crossword puzzle, and her thoughts returned to his flippant marriage proposal. Marriage obviously meant very little to him if he could offer it so casually. Why should that bother her so?

And why was she having such a hard time remembering that he wasn't a man, but a ghost? A ghost with no earthly future; a ghost whose marriage proposal meant nothing, regardless of his shallow motivation for making it. Sadness at that thought overwhelmed her.

Beside her, Dean, in his Mr. Rogers-style cardigan

and tassled loafers, took another huge, buttered handful from the popcorn bowl in his lap and munched in dazed contentment. Every now and then he'd let out a guffaw of laughter at the rerun of the "Donna Reed Show." Next would be "Father Knows Best." His enjoyment wasn't lessened at all by the fact that they'd seen every episode many times over.

Elissa bent her attention to her crossword puzzle, determined to expunge Jesse from her mind.

"Hot date, huh?" The comment, lightly spoken, held only a trace of wryness—but a heavy dose of resentment.

She stiffened. Jesse stood a few feet away, his booted feet spread in a classically virile stance, his thumbs hooked in the belt loops of his jeans, his gaze centered on her.

After a quick glance at Dean, who was still occupied with his television and popcorn, Elissa forced her attention back to her crossword puzzle, reminding herself that no matter what Jesse did, she'd ignore him. She read the first clue to the puzzle—one, across.

"I'm sorry I said that Dean had sex in mind when he brought you those roses," said Jesse. "I apologize if I...cheapened the gesture."

Elissa read the clue to her puzzle again, but couldn't quite focus on its meaning. She moved on to the next.

"Guess I just didn't like the idea of another man bringing you roses."

The print swam before her eyes. She wouldn't look at him. She swore she wouldn't.

He ambled closer, until his legs and thighs encased in worn denim intruded into her peripheral vision. He leaned one hip lazily against an armchair. "But you weren't quite right when you said I can't think past my zipper."

A dull heat crept into her cheeks, and a crushing witticism sprang to her tongue. She longed to barb him with her retort, but Dean sat fairly close beside her on the sofa.

As much as she tried to resist, Jesse's gaze drew hers—too compelling to ignore—and held her with a seriousness that took her breath away. "The truth is," he whispered gruffly, "I can't think past *you*."

Warmth pulsated through her.

"You believe that I made love to you that night, then went overseas without giving you another thought. That our lovemaking meant nothing to me." He sank down into the armchair, his knees apart, his forearms resting across them, his eyes now level with hers. "That just ain't so."

The heated sincerity in his stare blinded her to everything but him. She felt herself sinking deeper and deeper into another dimension. A dimension of emotion, of undiluted need. "What about you, Elissa?" he rasped. "How did you feel about our night together? Did it mean anything to you other than a good time?"

"Of course it did!" The low cry rushed from her lips before she could prevent it.

Dean cocked her an asking glance.

"I'm just...just trying to figure out this crossword puzzle," she uttered lamely. She needn't have worried. His attention immediately bounced back to the screen—and to the remote control he kept poised to fend off commercials.

"Tell me, Elissa," Jesse persisted, his gaze beseeching her with a dark magnetism, "what did it mean to you, that night we...found each other?"

*Everything*, she thought. Moisture coated her eyes. Here she was, fighting back tears and proclamations of love, after swearing to ignore him! She had to find more strength than this. She had to harden her heart. In desperation, she scribbled on the corner of her crossword puzzle, *Can't talk now*. With a sideways glance at an impervious Dean, she tipped the page to an angle for Jesse to see.

He read her message, and his gaze entwined with hers. "If our lovemaking meant anything to you, anything at all, you *will* talk now. And you'll tell Dean that I'm here."

Her lips parted in dismay. Again, she put her pencil to the page and wrote, *He might call too much attention to you*.

"I'm not afraid of Dean or anything he can do."

*I am*, she scribbled, underlining the words.

"Afraid that you'll lose him?"

She battled her inclination to tell him he was wrong. She wasn't afraid of losing Dean; she was afraid of losing Jesse.

"You don't love him, Elissa," he swore with a soft harshness. "If you did, you wouldn't have gone to bed with me. Not the first time, and not the second." In a scalding whisper, he added, "You might not know me, but I know you." Anguish glinted deep within his stare and touched her heart.

*Why do you want Dean to know you're here?* she wrote.

He read the question, and when he lifted his eyes again, the anguish had vanished, leaving only stark, gray ice. "We have things to settle, Dean and I."

His tone, his demeanor, the tense lines of his body, all communicated a threat that scared Elissa. What did he mean to do, and why? *Leave us alone, Jesse,* she wrote, hoping that by some miracle he'd listen.

When he'd read her reply, he drew in a long, quiet breath. Then he plied her with a look of utter disappointment—and an odd resignation that pierced her. "Is that what you want? *Is it?*"

Even before the question had fully registered, his presence changed. He began to fade. Before her very eyes, his image lost its vividness, and then its solidity, until it wavered like a hologram, transparent and surreal.

"Jesse!" she cried, reaching for him.

And then he was gone. Vanished.

She leaped to the armchair where he'd been sitting and groped the air, desperate to pull him back. "Oh, Jesse, Jesse, I didn't mean—"

"Elissa?" The word was a sharp admonishment as well as a question. She turned to find Dean staring at her with an astonished look. "What in heaven's name—? Had you fallen asleep? Were you dreaming?"

Perched on one knee at the edge of the armchair, she gazed at him in mute agony, a sob lodged in her throat. "No. No, I wasn't dreaming."

"You were calling Jesse."

She searched wildly around the room, hoping against hope that he might still be there. But the resignation in his gaze remained vivid in her memory. She'd made a choice, and he had honored it. The sob worked its way from her throat to her lips. All he'd asked of her was honesty—to let Dean know he was there. Could that request have had something to do with his final goal? If so, she had failed him miserably.

Coming to a decision, she returned to her place on the

sofa and faced Dean. "There's something you should know. Something I should have told you earlier."

He frowned and lifted a shoulder. "What?"

"Jesse..." Her throat closed at the mention of his name, and she struggled to clear it. After a moment, she managed to say, "Jesse has been here."

Dean's sandy-brown eyebrows scrunched together. "Of course he's been here. He lived here."

"No, I mean recently. This evening. He was...with us."

Dean barked an uncomfortable little laugh, as if she'd made a joke he didn't quite understand. With a decisive move—one that proclaimed the seriousness of the subject—he aimed the remote control and lowered the volume of the television. "Surely you don't mean that literally?"

"Yes, actually, I do. His ghost has been haunting me." As her words sank in, Dean's brows rose. Determinedly, she pressed on, "I told you about the first time I saw him—the morning of his death. He appeared again after his funeral, when I came to look at his house. And quite a few times since. That's why I'm here. To communicate with him."

He stared at her. "You mean you really believe Jesse is here," he summarized in droll amazement, "in this room with us, right now?"

"No." The word sounded bleak, even to her own ears, and she resented the relief that spread over Dean's face. "He left a few minutes ago."

"Good Lord, listen to yourself, Elissa! Babbling about ghosts and communicating with spirits!"

"I know it sounds crazy, but—"

"You're obviously going through denial." He reached out and drew her closer to him on the sofa with a gentle yet insistent arm around her. Concern shone in his pale blue eyes. "I'm sorry I didn't realize sooner how...attached...you'd grown to Jesse." His voice, though warm, resonated with a undeniable edge of bitterness. "I guess I should have seen it—your touchiness every time his name was mentioned, your certainty that he was alive."

She pulled away from the patronizing embrace. "I knew you wouldn't believe me." With forlorn hope, she called out to the room at large, "Jesse, if you're here, I could use some help."

"You could definitely use some help," muttered Dean, his stare laden with disapproval. "You have to stop this craziness, Elissa. Now, let's look at things rationally. The first time you saw his...ghost...was while your day-care charges were sleeping, wasn't it?"

"Yes." She wondered what that had to do with anything.

"So you were probably napping yourself and didn't even realize it. You just dreamed that Jesse was there."

"It wasn't like that. I walked around and talked to him. Argued with him, for heaven's sake. I've seen him a dozen times since then—spent whole days with him." Since she'd gone this far, she decided she might as well sound completely bonkers. "He has extraordinary powers now. He can appear and disappear. He can walk through walls. He even slammed a door without touching it."

The quality of Dean's stare changed—from unrelenting disbelief to what Elissa swore was uncertainty. As if her last statement held more validity than the rest.

His lips tightened to a thin white line, and his eyes narrowed. "Did Jesse, or maybe my mother, say anything to you about his...well, his talent?"

"Talent? No. What talent?"

He hesitated, as if debating the wisdom of telling. "It wasn't a normal skill. It never did anybody any good."

"What was it?" she demanded.

Looking sullen, Dean took a deep breath, rose from the sofa and paced across the living room. "When Jesse was a kid, sometimes he'd get angry and things would...well, happen. Doors would slam, things would fall off shelves."

She stared at him incredulously.

"If you've already heard about that," continued Dean, "your subconscious mind probably twisted it out of proportion and now you're having nightmares. Waking nightmares."

"You're telling me that Jesse moved things with his mind *before* he died?" The thought stirred a memory of Professor Lehmberg's theories. Something about well-trained psychic minds gaining even more power in the spiritual realm...

"Damn it, Elissa, I wish you'd never met him," swore Dean. "Jesse always meant trouble for me. I knew when he showed up at my door that I shouldn't let him near you. He always drew the attention to himself, no matter where we were. Everyone saw only Jesse." Realizing he'd gotten sidetracked, he ranted, "He was the devil's spawn, Elissa. All the girls went crazy over him. Even the boys followed him around like he was some hero. No one knew him like I did. He took real pleasure in hurting people...especially me."

Resentment stirred in Elissa. In the past when Dean had told her negative things about Jesse, she'd taken it as a friend's warning against a heartbreaker. Now his words seemed only malicious. "I don't believe that Jesse would intentionally hurt anyone."

Dean glared at her as if she'd gone mad. "And I don't believe your blind defense of him! I'd have thought that you, of all people, could see past his muscular physique and handsome mug to the real person. He's the by-product of a rape. And from things I've heard, he's a chip off the old block. He himself wasn't above forcing a girl now and then."

"You must have been misinformed about that." Her voice shook, but she managed to keep it level. "One thing I know for sure is that Jesse's no rapist. Both times I was with him, he made a point to stop and ask my permission, even when I was on the brink of...of..." she halted, appalled at what she'd been about to tell Dean.

"On the brink of what?" The curious prodding came not from Dean, but from the very air around her. And the voice, the deep, vibrant voice, was the one she'd been longing to hear.

Awash in relief that he'd returned—and embarrassment at what he'd heard her say—Elissa felt color heat its way up her neck to the very roots of her hair. "Never mind. That's not important now." And with unfocused eyes, she spoke to the vibrant air, "But I finally understand what is." She directed her gaze back to Dean, who obviously hadn't heard Jesse's remark. "Just rest assured that Jesse Garrett is far from being a rapist."

Dean's thin lips twisted. "Did you say, *both* times you were with him? When could you possibly have been with him a second time? Unless we're counting a post-mortem visit."

Her warm color refused to recede. "I'm sorry, Dean, but that's none of your business." The question probably wouldn't have bothered her so much if Jesse hadn't been listening to every word. "Jesse, if you'll just make your presence known, this confrontation will go much smoother."

*Can't.* The reply was too quiet to be called a whisper. It was more of a thought that shimmered through her mind.

Dean stared at her in horror. "Do you really believe that you're conversing with Jesse now?"

"No, I wouldn't call it conversing. It seems he needs more rest to build up his energy to a sufficient level."

"Rest? He needs more rest? For God's sake, he's dead! How much more rest can he get?"

Tired of Dean's negativity, she spouted, "Dead is as dead does!"

Burying his head in his hands, Dean sank down onto the sofa. "You're cracking up, Elissa. Cracking up over Jesse." When he lifted his head, his eyes were shiny with tears. "He's not worth it, I'm telling you! Don't you remember what he did to you? He screwed you, then took off, without even answering your letters." The air around them suddenly chilled, deeply and dramatically. Elissa felt it and shivered, but Dean was too caught up in his distress to notice. "You should have heard him when he called me from those brothels in Asia."

*Brothels?* The word exploded in her mind like a tossed hand grenade.

She bit her lip in consternation. "Are you sure he was calling from brothels?"

"Hell, yes. He told me!" insisted Dean. "I heard the women giggling in the background. You didn't really think that a stud like Jesse would go for even a few days without having himself serviced, did you?"

Again, a silent reply ripped through her: *Self-service only, that whole damned year. While I was thinking about you*. Elissa could virtually hear the growl in Jesse's voice; see the anger in his eyes, invisible though he was. Her blood warmed to him.

"You must have misinterpreted the situation," she said to Dean. "He was probably calling from a restaurant or bar."

*I made no calls to Dean.*

Elissa froze. No calls? He'd made no calls? But how could that be? Surely Dean wouldn't have lied...would he? Jumped to false conclusions, yes, but not lied.

"I told you what Jesse said when I mentioned your pregnancy," reminded Dean, a brutal edge to voice. "He laughed. Then he said, 'Just because I play a game of pool doesn't mean I want to lug the pool table around with me.'"

The plunge in temperature this time was too severe to be ignored by even the angriest man. Dean shivered, looked around and rubbed his arms. "It's getting cold in here," he muttered. "Damned cold."

Elissa was more mindful of a tension in the air, an odd, watchful tension, as if Jesse were waiting. Wondering whose side she would believe...

She gazed keenly at Dean, who was now chafing his hands to warm them. Could he have told her such destructive lies at a time when she'd been in desperate emotional need?

"Dean," she said quietly, "that address you gave me for Jesse. Where did you get it?"

His gaze jerked back to hers. "Where did I get it? From my address book. Jesse's mother gave me that address."

Wrapping her arms around herself to fight off the bitter cold and the trembling that had taken hold of her, she asked, "Jesse didn't give you an address? A more recent one?"

Dean frowned. His neck and face slowly turned an unbecoming red. "No." The word sounded suspiciously tentative. "I guess he just didn't think of it. He knows I'm not one for writing letters."

"May I see your wallet?"

"My wallet?" He blinked. "Whatever for?"

"Humor me, Dean."

"But I don't understand why—" He grabbed for his back pocket, too late. His wallet had slipped through his hand and fluttered to the floor. With a start, he stared down at it in disbelief.

Elissa knelt and picked up the wallet that had fallen open on the Persian carpet. She gathered the folded money and business cards that had rained out.

Dean stuttered, "H-h-how did...how did that..."

"Jesse obviously wants me to see it." Her voice had grown cool and curt. She took no pity on Dean despite the little-boy look of bewilderment on his stunned face.

"You did that, didn't you?" he whispered. "You have the same psychic power as Jesse. I never knew you could do that. I don't think you should. I hated it when he made things move...hated it...."

Elissa ignored his flustered rambling. One by one, she flicked through his business cards until she found his hairstylist's—Pierre's House of Beauty. With a heaviness already weighing down her heart, she turned the card over. She knew full well what she'd find.

"An army base in Asia." She raised demanding eyes to him. "Whose address is this, Dean? It's not the one you gave me for Jesse."

"I...I forgot all about that address. It was so early in the morning when he wrote it."

"You lied to me." Her faint voice shook with sad, incredulous discovery.

"Lied to you? I didn't lie to you!"

"Things might have been so different for Jesse and me."

"Damn it, Elissa, he wasn't good enough for you."

"I should have been the one to judge that."

"I was protecting you! I love you. Jesse never did."

"At least he never lied to me."

"You only met him once."

"And you meant to keep it that way, didn't you."

With a curse, Dean grabbed her by the shoulders and dragged her to him. "I know what you're missing," he fumed, "and it's not Jesse." Twining his arms forcibly around her, he panted, "He's not the only one who can give it to you."

Startled, she wrenched away from his desperate attempts to kiss her and shoved at his chest. He staggered backward with much more force than her push had warranted. In fact, he crashed against the end table and flipped over it, as if a huge, angry man had slung him there.

*As if.*

Stunned, Dean pulled himself to his feet, too outraged to question the strength of her shove. "It's my turn, Elissa," he ranted, beating at his thin chest with one fist. His face and neck had turned a blotchy red and sweat trickled from his forehead. "It's way past time for my turn. I was good to you. I was willing to marry you even after your scandal. I was ready to take in Jesse's bastard!"

Elissa gasped as the razor-sharp hurt of betrayal sliced through her. He was talking about Cody, her baby, with a malice that shocked her.

"You like it this way, don't you?" he spat, advancing

with a resentful gleam in his eyes. "Rough and dirty must be your style—or you wouldn't have jumped into the sack with Jesse. I knew you for years, Elissa. Years! Jesse was a damn stranger. So why the hell did you go to bed with him, but not with me? How could Jesse's touch turn you into a—"

He never got the chance to finish. He was jerked up by the throat—as evidenced by choking noises and a gaping mouth—and slammed backward against the stairwell wall so hard that pictures jumped and crashed to the floor.

Dean hung there choking, pinned to the wall with his tassled loafers kicking uselessly above the floor. Doors all over the house slammed, lights flickered and a wintry wind blustered around the living room.

The vase of roses Dean had brought her leaped from the mantel and shattered, strewing the flowers across the hearth. The popcorn bowl flipped off the sofa and sprayed kernels into the wind, which howled like a pack of banshees.

"Stop it, Jesse!" cried Elissa, her hair whipping furiously around her as popcorn bounced off the walls and flower petals fluttered before her eyes. "Just stop it this instant!"

The commotion kept on. Books fell off shelves, vertical blinds clanged together, and Dean's head banged violently against the wall as he choked to a ghastly purple.

Elissa crossed her arms, lifted her chin and tapped her slippered foot. "Go ahead, Jesse. Kill him. But if you do, I won't speak to you."

It took a moment, but the chaos gradually lessened. First the wind died down, then the lights stopped flickering. Doors quit banging; books stopped leaping from their shelves. And finally Dean was lowered to the floor.

He collapsed there, gulping for breath and trembling. Wild-eyed, he gazed around the room. "It *is* you, isn't it, Jesse," he squeaked when he finally regained his voice. "Even death couldn't keep you in your place."

A gold letter opener rose up off the cluttered floor, launched across the living room and stuck in the wall beside his head, vibrating with an audible *twang*.

Dean whimpered and cowered away from the dagger like weapon. "There's no reason for you to be mad, Jesse. You should be grateful. Grateful!" He took a moment to swallow as he inched his way along the wall toward the front door. "You told me to watch out for Elissa until you got back. That's all I'm doing—watching out for her. Who else is going to take care of her now that you're dead?"

The coat-closet door opened and slammed with eloquent fury. Elissa winced.

"Stop deluding yourself, Dean," she said. "I've been the one taking care of *you*." With cool arrogance, she then sauntered closer, the frigidity of the room matching the state of her heart. "I thought you were a friend," she said. "You hurt me. Deeply. But I thank God for that. Because now you'll never get the opportunity to hurt my son the way you and your pompous family hurt Jesse." Clasping her trembling hands behind her, she nodded toward the door. "Now, you'd better get the hell out of here...before I let Jesse decapitate you."

With a grateful sob, Dean scrambled to his feet and loped toward the foyer. As he neared it, he either performed a remarkable leap in a uniquely arched position, or an invisible foot connected with his backside and booted him out the door.

## 11

"SHHH, IT'S OKAY, CODY. Everything's okay." Elissa hugged the wailing baby fiercely to her. The noise of banging doors and shattering glass undoubtedly had woken him. Cuddling him against her shoulder, she rocked and hummed and pressed her cheek against his sleep-warmed head, savoring his baby scent.

She loved him so much. Why hadn't she seen the danger she'd almost subjected him to? If she'd married Dean, Cody would have grown up with the same steady diet of poison that Jesse had been fed as a child. For all his caring ways, Dean had resented Cody with a spite that shocked her. He'd called him "Jesse's bastard."

Pain shot through her—not for herself, but for her sweet, innocent son; that anyone would scorn him, devalue him as a person, before his personality had even formed, before he had a chance to develop a defense against the hatefulness.

How had Jesse prevailed against such malice, aimed at him from birth? She thought back to his funeral and his aunt's viciousness, his mother's lack of grief. The pain in her intensified—this time for Jesse. "Oh, God, Jesse, hadn't your own mother defended you against the family's spite?"

*My mother's not to blame.* The quick, silent reply came

to her as clearly as spoken words. Elissa glanced around the darkened bedroom, but saw no one.

"Not to blame?" she repeated in a pained whisper. "How could any mother *not* defend her child against hatred? How could she let them say you were born from bad seed, with bad blood...."

"She didn't understand any of that." This time, the words were spoken aloud, quietly, from the direction of the doorway. "As an adult, I came to realize that."

"What do you mean, she didn't understand?" Elissa continued to search the shadows, desperate for the sight of him.

"She had a severe case of scarlet fever as a child. She'd been exceptionally bright before that, from what I gathered. A writer, a poet. But the fever...well..." Sadness hung heavy in the darkness. "She believed whatever my aunt told her."

Elissa wanted to enfold him in the same kind of hug she now held Cody in. She sensed within his spirit a raw, gaping wound, and wanted so much to heal it. Through a tightened throat, she asked, "Then how did you turn out so good?"

Silence answered her—and Jesse materialized in the shadows near the foot of the crib, a stunned look in his cloud gray eyes. Wariness gradually crept into his stare, as if he was waiting for the inevitable put-down....

She realized then that she had wronged him far worse than Dean and his family. She'd fallen in love with him, given him a son, and still refused to see the honor in him.

He had asked Dean to watch out for her until he returned from his overseas duty. All he'd received in return had been her brief, cold letters notifying him of their baby—and demanding he relinquish his parental

rights. Even so, he had provided for Cody and her in his
will. Death itself hadn't stopped him from coming to
see them, trying to resolve the conflict she had created.
She'd sent him away even then, her mind set against
him by gossip. Why had she allowed herself to be so
swayed? Why hadn't she listened to her own heart?

She listened to it now. "You *are* good, Jesse," she
swore fervently. "I'd want no other father for my
child."

Silence hummed between them. And Jesse's image
grew bright—intensely so, as if some electrical surge
had increased his energy tenfold. But too soon, the
brightness faded. His image wavered, and he disappeared into the bedroom shadows.

Elissa's throat constricted with torturous self-blame.
Her blindfold had been ripped away too late.

She hugged her baby, who slept soundly in her arms.
She needed the comfort of his warmth, his closeness.
Jesse's blood ran through his veins, and though she'd
always loved her son beyond limitation, his parentage
now filled her with a bittersweet pride and tenderness.

Cody squirmed in her arms; she'd been holding him
too tightly. She bent over the crib to lower him into it.

A low whisper tore from the shadows, "No, bring
him."

She lifted her eyes and saw no one. "Bring him—?"

"In here."

A baby blanket rose from the crib, clutched by invisible hands. She followed it out into the corridor, down
the hall and into the master bedroom. The blanket
wafted down onto a pallet of large floor pillows that
had been arranged in front of the bedroom hearth. As
she stood watching from the doorway, a spark flared in
the fireplace, and a flame burst from the kindling. Be-

hind an antique fire screen, a small fire soon crackled and danced.

"Come here, Elissa." The quiet invitation drew her attention to the floor pillows where Jesse reclined, solidly visible in the golden firelight, leaning on one elbow beside the outspread baby blanket. "Lay him down here."

Slowly she approached, breathing in the redolence of polished hardwood flooring, firewood and Jesse's subtle aftershave. Folding her jeans-clad legs beneath her, she sat on the pillows and nestled her baby on the blanket beside his father. A potent contentment soon replaced the chill that had seeped into her bones.

Feeling unaccountably breathless as she watched Jesse gaze down at his slumbering son, she managed to whisper, "It's good to see you, Jesse." The cliché took on a whole new meaning. He smiled slightly in acknowledgment and she breathed easier. She'd been so afraid of never making him smile again.

"It would be good to touch you," he said.

Longing rushed through her as their gazes locked. She wanted his touch. She wanted to be in his arms, to assuage the ache in her soul with the awesome power of his lovemaking. "We can't," she whispered.

"We will." He made no move to touch her.

Unable to contain her guilt a moment longer, she said, "I'm sorry, Jesse. I wronged you so badly."

"I'd rather be wronged by you than loved by anyone else."

Though her heart swelled with fierce love for him, she wouldn't be distracted from her apology. "I doubted every word you said. I believed Dean without question. When I think of the mistake I might have made, allowing him to act as a father to Cody!" She shuddered. "There's no telling the psychological damage he would have inflicted. How could I have been so blind?" A possibility, a likelihood, then struck her. "Is that why you came back, Jesse? To show me Dean's true nature?"

"I'd like to say it was, but I'd be lying. Dean had me fooled, too. I thought we were family."

Although his expression hadn't changed, her sympathy went out to him. She'd forgotten that he, too, had suffered a betrayal, perhaps worse than hers.

"I came back for you." His voice softened with a sensual gruffness. "Dean was wrong when he said I never loved you. I did. From our very first conversation."

Her lips parted in surprise. "Our first conversation? But I...I didn't say much." She'd been awed by him that entire evening—by his masculine beauty, yes, but more by the raw, sensual power that had drawn her irresistibly to him.

"You might not have said much in words." His stare warmed her with its heat. "But we didn't need words then. I think we do now. I love you, Elissa. Marry me."

Emotion lifted her heart, then twisted it painfully. She was elated that he loved her; astonished that he could, after her hateful distrust. And she was agonized that their love could never be. She wanted to say yes, to spend the rest of her life with him, to disregard the fact that he was visible only to her, and then only at certain times. But she knew better than to hope that a future together was even a remote possibility. He belonged elsewhere.

"Don't answer me," he said curtly, "until there's not a doubt left in you."

Tears slowly filled her eyes. She had never loved him more. "Jesse, it's not a question of doubting love—mine or yours. We can't possibly marry. You have no future in this world. You died in that plane crash. You should be headed toward your...destiny."

Annoyance flickered across his rugged face. "Let's not start with that nonsense again."

"I wish it were nonsense, but it's not. You're dead." Seeing that she was getting nowhere with this tactic, she asked, "When you experienced those blackouts, did you see anything you didn't quite understand?"

"Like what?"

She didn't want to tell him. She didn't want him to leave her. But what choice did she have? "In the near-death experiences that have been recorded, most have one thing in common—a tunnel that the spirit seems to travel through. There's a light at the end of that tunnel. A parapsychologist told me that earthbound spirits should be directed toward that light. Have you...seen it?"

"No, I haven't seen any damn tunnel or any damn light." He paused, then slanted her a considering look, as if hesitating to confide in her. After a moment he murmured, "I do remember something about the downed flight, though. You know, the plane crash that...*killed* me."

She winced at the sarcasm and chose to ignore it. "What do you remember?"

"I remember the plane taking a dive and panic breaking out among the men. Then earsplitting noise and smoke and pain. It seemed to go on forever."

"Oh, Jesse!"

"And then there's snatches of other memories that I can't quite put together. Blurred faces, babbled voices. I thought I heard the word *dakrah*."

"*Dakrah?*" she repeated, mystified.

"It's a word I learned on an undercover mission two years ago, when I worked in an Asian village. We needed information about a terrorist, and I was the only one who spoke the language well enough to get by."

"What does the word mean?"

A muscle moved in his jaw. "It means dying." After a grim moment of reflection, he shrugged. "But then I also remember hearing Colonel Atkinson, shortly after that."

"Colonel Atkinson?"

"Yeah." With a half frown, half smile, Jesse shook his head. "The colonel said, 'I'll eat green grits for you, son.'"

"Green grits!"

"It's a private joke between us. Has to do with a Saint Patrick's Day we spent here in Savannah. He could take the green beer—plenty of it—but not the green grits."

"Oh, Jesse, it sounds like you were dreaming. Delirious, probably." *On your deathbed.*

His stare seemed to probe her thoughts. "You really think I'm dead, don't you. What the hell can I do to prove I'm not?" He reached for her, and she drew away.

"Don't risk touching me, Jesse! I'm afraid that if you do, you'll disappear again, before we even have a chance to—" She broke off midsentence.

He wasn't listening. He had drawn back his hand and now frowned down at it as he examined his little finger.

"Is something wrong with your hand?" She resisted the urge to take it in her own to better see it. She couldn't touch him. She dared not endanger whatever life force he had left. "Does it hurt?"

"No, it doesn't hurt, but—" He balled up his fist, then

slowly released it, watching his little finger. "My finger's been giving me trouble. It's numb."

"What do you mean, numb? Like, pins and needles?"

"Like, no feeling in it at all."

His explanation sent a shard of fear through her. Professor Lehmberg had theorized, *"Maybe he'll simply cease to exist."* Elissa's panic flared. No. She couldn't bear to believe it. "Maybe you hurt your finger when you were choking Dean."

"I did that with my mind, not my hand."

"Oh. Well, maybe you jammed your finger when you fell off my bed the other morning."

"No, I remember it bugging me before that...when I changed your flat tire."

"Could it be from punching those men in that roadside fight?"

"I hit 'em with my right hand, not my left."

A dark foreboding gripped her. Would he gradually lose *all* feeling? "Oh, Jesse, please listen to me! It's starting to happen, just like Dr. Lehmberg warned it might. This is serious, *real* serious."

"My finger?" He let out a brief laugh. "Over the last fifteen years, I've been shot more times than I care to remember, holed up in deserts and jungles for months on end, chained in foreign prisons with electrodes attached to my—" he stopped. His lips tightened. "Let's just say that I'm not going to die over a numb pinkie."

Stunned by his casual revelations, Elissa wanted to take him in her arms and blot out those painful memories with good, loving ones. But it was too late for that.

"Jesse, that numb pinkie might be just the start. The longer you stay trapped from your destiny, the more you'll suffer. Please open your mind to the possibility that I'm right."

The passionate concern in those brown eyes almost made Jesse forgive her for not saying that she loved him. Almost, but not quite. He wouldn't let her get away without saying it. "If someone told you that you were dead, would you believe 'em?"

"No," she admitted, "but that's an entirely different matter. I'm not invisible!" Expelling a harried breath, she raked loose, sable dark waves from her face and smoothed them behind one ear. "Humor me, then, Jesse," she implored in the low, smoky voice that always stirred him to thoughts of lovemaking. "There's obviously some goal you haven't attained, some need left unfulfilled that's very important to you. Think what it might be."

Only one came to mind. *He had to make her his.* He had to make Elissa Sinclair love him as he loved her—eternally, unconditionally, and at any cost.

But of course, he also had a whole lifetime of other, less compelling business that he fully intended to handle. He damned sure wasn't dead. If he were, he'd be the first to admit it.

"Can't you think of anything?" she prompted. "Any goal that you feel passionate about achieving?"

"Just one." Straining to resist the powerful urge to pull her into his arms, he whispered, "I would defy death itself for a lifetime of loving you."

Her stare—her passionate, caring stare—darkened with a curious emotion, the last one he expected to see there. Alarm. "Me?" she breathed. "I'm keeping you here?" With an almost inaudible sob, she wrenched her gaze away from his, gathered up the sleeping infant and stumbled toward the door.

"Elissa!" he called.

But she didn't stop. She didn't even glance back. The

door to her room across the hall shut. The lock clicked into place.

Astonished by her reaction, Jesse stared off in the direction she had fled. He had opened his heart to her, as he had with no one else in his life. And she had refused him. Locked her door against him.

Why? How could the need, the desire, the love that consumed him be completely one-sided? And what, Jesse wondered, made her think that a mere locked door would keep him out?

He rose to follow her, but the weariness set in. It felt deeper and more debilitating than ever.

SHE HAD INTENDED TO GO—to pack her bags, bundle Cody up in his blankets and drive far, far away from here. But common sense prevailed before she'd packed a single bag. She couldn't outrun Jesse. He had appeared at her house, at an isolated roadside spot, in a hotel room and near the river. He had accompanied her into town; he had spirited Cody away to his backyard garden. Where could she possibly go that Jesse couldn't follow?

Even now, she kept glancing around the bedroom, waiting for him to appear. Oddly enough, he did not.

With a sense of impending doom, she gave up her plan to leave, changed into her nightgown and slipped beneath the bedcovers, her misery roiling within her. *She* was the one keeping Jesse trapped in this mortal world. Her love for him, her need to be with him, had obviously spanned the miles—and the boundaries of life and death—to hold him back from that final trek to the other side.

Even if she hadn't actually summoned him away from the beckoning light, she had given him reason to stay with her. She'd laughed with him, cried over him, made love to him. She'd given him a son. Dangerous things to do with a man like Jesse. He was simply too strong-willed to let a good thing pass. And their love *was* a good thing, the very best thing that she'd ever found in her life. Or rather, it could have been...if only he were still alive.

But he was not. And it wasn't only Jesse denying that fact. She herself had not accepted it. Even now, as she lay agonizing in his guest room, knowing that her love was destroying him, she wanted to hold him again. She wanted to love him.

She had to fight that love. She had to deny its very existence, even to herself. Only then did she have a chance of saving Jesse, of motivating him to leave.

Hardening her resolve to send him away if he should appear, Elissa lay on her side, her hand tucked beneath her cheek on the pillow, her eyes resolutely closed. She had to sleep. She would need her wits about her tomorrow. First thing in the morning, she'd pack her bags and leave for home. If Jesse followed, she'd make him wish he hadn't.

A clock downstairs chimed twelve, a lone dog howled somewhere in the distance, and the big old house creaked around her. Slowly, Elissa drifted into slumber.

It was sometime later, hours, maybe, when movement in the bed disrupted her sleep, and her eyes fluttered open.

"Don't open your eyes." The whisper rushed across her ear from behind, and she became aware of a warm, male body against her back. She knew instantly who it was, and before her mind could censure her response, her heart rejoiced.

"Close your eyes, Elissa," he commanded softly. His hand brushed down over her eyelids and forced them closed. "You wouldn't be able to see me right now, and I'd rather not end up on the floor." His wry comment reminded her of the fright she'd suffered earlier in the week, finding him invisible in her bed. "It seems that if I don't waste energy on trying to appear," he explained, "I can...touch you."

She realized with a little shock that it was true—he was touching her. Yet she felt no hellish force prying them apart, no psychic current running through them.

His hand drifted away from her eyes, which remained obediently closed, and he pulled her closer, his arm around her waist. "I'd give up visibility forever if it's the only way I can hold you."

Longing coursed through her as his solid, muscular form cradled her, their bodies fitting spoonlike. Sensuality bloomed within her, its roots reaching deep and low.

"Jesse," she implored, struggling to resist its sweet lure, "I'm leaving tomorrow."

"Why?" Though no more than a drawn-out whisper, the word resounded with disappointment, frustration, opposition.

"To get help. Professional help. I...I don't know how to deal with a...a ghost." She felt his body tense—as if from a physical blow—and she had to force herself to continue. "I'm going to hire a channeler, or whatever kind of psychic might be able to guide you to the 'other side.'"

He cursed softly and thoroughly. The bed creaked, and with an abrupt movement, he rolled her onto her back. From the proximity of his voice and the way his breath fanned her cheek, she knew he had braced himself above her. She kept her eyes closed. She didn't want to replace the comforting image she held in her mind's eye with the frightening reality—an angry, invisible Jesse.

"Damn it, Elissa," he swore, "I'm not a ghost."

"Then why can't I open my eyes?"

"Go ahead and open them. But I don't have the energy to appear. Not if I want to touch you. And I do want to touch you," he added on a gruff whisper.

"If you're not a ghost, then there's only one thing you could be." She steeled herself against the inevitable pain. "You must be a figment of my imagination. A fantasy conjured up by grief. In which case—" she choked out the words, holding back tears "—I'd better see a grief counselor, or maybe a shrink."

A sharply indrawn breath told her the words had hit him hard. After a tense moment, heat tingled over her; the dry, unnatural heat powered by his anger. Ever so softly, he scoffed, "A figment of your imagination, am I?"

"You must be."

His muscles shifted with sudden purpose, and before she knew what he was doing, he'd leaped from the bed and scooped her up into his arms. She cried out, her eyes flew open, and sheer darkness spun alarmingly around her. She shut her eyes and clung to the warm, muscular neck, shoulders and chest that she wasn't able to see.

"I'm taking you to my bed," he uttered hoarsely, "where you belong."

"I don't belong there," she said with an anguished sob.

"I want to remember you there, anyway."

In a few long strides, he'd crossed the hall and

reached his bedroom. Above her riotous heartbeats she heard the crackle of the fire in the hearth, felt its gentle warmth. When Jesse halted, she peeked down to see the bedcovers of his huge pine bed peel magically back from the pillows.

She closed her eyes again as she tumbled down onto the mattress. Jesse swiftly joined her there, his bare, iron-strong legs, arms and torso sliding over hers, trapping her neatly beneath him.

"Get off me," she demanded between clenched teeth, struggling to free herself from his sleekly muscled body.

"Are you talking to me?" he asked in a ragged whisper, his breath warm against her mouth and chin. "Or to yourself?"

She understood then. He intended to force her into acknowledging that he was certainly more than a product of her mind. "Maybe I *am* talking to myself," she retorted. "I must be delusional—wrestling with a man who isn't even here." To prove her point, she defiantly opened her eyes.

But he *was* there, heart-stoppingly real—all human, all male, and furious as a thundercloud. His silver-hot gaze fused with hers, and traitorous joy sparked in her heart. She'd wanted so much to see him, to hold him....

"If I'm just your imagination, Elissa," he whispered as he lowered his dark, glowering face, "then let your imagination run wild."

His mouth accosted hers then with persuasive insistence—laving, tasting and probing until the kiss slanted and flowed. Caught up in the sensuous revelry, she kissed him back with a vengeance. If this was madness, then mad she wanted to be.

His muscles hardened in immediate response and

erotic heat flared between them. His fingers worked at the buttons of her nightgown, then tugged at the interfering fabric until he had stripped it completely off of her. He then drew her against him with another kiss, this one deeper and slower.

Elissa lost herself in the feel of his skin pressing against hers, the smooth brawn of his muscles bunching beneath her palms, the exquisite heat of his mouth as it glided in a swirling path to her throat, to her breasts.

He worked his way steadily downward. She wove her fingers through his silky hair as he kissed her in provocative, lingering ways that made her tremble.

With his hands hard and controlling, he captured her mobile hips and laid siege. Every advance heightened her sublime sensitivity, until involuntary shuddering set in.

And then he stopped. Withdrew his mouth, his hands.

"Jesse," she breathed, "what are you—?"

He started again—a strategic attack, using every weapon in his arsenal this time. She gasped as his hardness probed, entered and slowly inched into her. The pleasure steadily compounded and grew acute. Too soon, he retreated.

Through a swelter of need, she cried in a tortured whisper, "Don't you dare stop!" Then with a breathless sob, she moaned, "You're driving me crazy...."

His body lunged across hers and he caught her hands above her head, pinning them against the mattress. With his gaze dark and determined, he thundered, "Who's driving you crazy, Elissa? *Who*?"

She knew she could distract him with moves of her own—moves that would drive all rational thought right out of his head. She saw the barely leashed desire straining behind the purpose in his steel gray eyes.

But that purpose stopped her. He wanted her to admit that he was real, and here, and loving her. That was one admission she couldn't make. She had to send him away before her love destroyed him.

Surly and hoarse, he demanded, "Who?"

She squared her jaw. "No one."

"No one?"

"No one."

His bottom lip curled, his hands tightened on her wrists. And slowly, intently, he rocked forward. His male hardness pushed in, completely in, filling her to capacity.

Pleasure radiated to every fiber of her being; pleasure, and the love she struggled to hide. He gave another smooth, hard thrust, his gaze locked intently on hers. She couldn't stop her body from meeting his thrusts, couldn't stop her gaze from dancing with his.

He released her wrists, braced himself on his knees, and deepened the penetration. His rhythm quickened, his urgency grew, until each gliding thrust lifted her hips off the bed.

"I want more from you," he growled, "and you know it."

She loved him too much to give it.

With a groan of desperation, he lowered his fevered body to hers, his hardness still throbbing inside her. His fingers slipped into her hair, his thumbs rested beside her mouth. "Believe in me, Elissa," he begged. And he kissed her with a deep, aching need.

She melted into his all-consuming kiss, undone by his ragged plea. Their arms coiled tightly around each other, their legs intertwined, and their bodies writhed in slow, sensual opposition.

Later, when the tremors of aftershock had subsided, Jesse whispered into her ear, "You love me, Elissa. I feel it."

She did love him, so much it hurt. So much that she couldn't fathom losing him. And though she felt as if she were ripping her own heart out, she whispered, "No, Jesse." The acute pain of those two words almost defeated her, but she had to persevere, for the sake of his very existence. She choked out the blackest lie of her entire life. "Whatever it is you think you feel, well—" she even managed a shrug "—it's just your imagination."

Suffocating bleakness overtook her as she disengaged herself from his embrace and edged away until she no longer touched him. She fully expected him to reach for her, to pull her back.

He did not.

She felt as though she'd never sleep again. But soon enough, a drugging slumber blotted out her anguish.

A similar lassitude overtook Jesse—similar in its narcotic effect, yet very different. Different also from the numbing weariness that had so often attacked him these past few weeks. This sleep submerged him into a pulsating darkness, then plunged him headlong into some vacuumlike abyss. He tried to fight it, but found he hadn't the energy—or the reason—to resist.

She had wanted him to leave her. The pain of that realization sapped his strength way more than anything so far. To find her, then to lose her, even as he held her in his arms and loved her with all his heart...

The pain grew into a live, gnawing force. The darkness hummed as he sped through it, hummed with an inhuman wailing. Gradually the wailing turned into a dull babble of voices. Though incoherent, they seemed to be calling to him, not by name, but unmistakably beckoning in tone. He strained against a blinding wind to see. Vague forms hovered around in the murky distance.

*Why had Elissa turned him away?* Had they been right, all those monsters of his youth, lurking in every darkness, taunting him with the likelihood that no one could ever love him? He hadn't known then exactly what he'd been missing. He hadn't known until she'd shown him.

The pain intensified.

The darkness narrowed, tunnellike.

He looked for it. He looked for the light.

# 12

SHE SHOT UP IN BED with a violent start, her heart thundering. She had to hurry. *Hurry.*

In panic, she gazed around until she recognized her surroundings—Jesse's bedroom. The sun hadn't yet begun to filter through the morning darkness. The terrible urgency pumping through her veins had to have been caused by a nightmare.

Weakly, she leaned against the pillows. She couldn't remember the dream. And though she knew that there was no reason to leap from the bed and scramble into her clothes, the urgency continued to drum in her heart. *Hurry. Hurry.* But to where, to do what?

With a trembling hand, she turned on the bedside lamp. The fire in the hearth had dwindled to ashes and chill bumps had risen across her skin. Her nightgown lay on the floor, and only a linen sheet covered her. The soreness of her muscles, the swollen feel of her lips, and the musky male scent of Jesse that clung to her skin brought back vivid memories of last night. Jesse, though, was gone.

She stared at the indentation in the pillow where his head had rested. She was alone, she knew. He wouldn't reappear, or whisper to her from thin air, or even watch her from some mystical vantage point. He had finally left her.

She should be glad that he had gone, that she had

sent him in the right direction. Instead, she felt only an aching sense of loss…and this peculiar urgency.

It had to be a reaction to his departure. How *would* she face the prospect of living her entire life without love, without passion, without laughter? Without Jesse? She certainly couldn't face that prospect right now. The pain of it nearly doubled her over.

She gave in to tears—silent, anguished tears—for the man she had sent away. For the bleak, empty future she faced without him. After a while, when she'd cried herself out, she realized the urgent feeling that had awoken her remained. As if someone essential to her was in mortal danger.

Unnerved, she hurried from the bed to Jesse's closet and, looking for a robe, rifled through his shirts, pants and military uniforms. The sight of his clothes pierced her with fresh anguish, but she couldn't wallow in her grief. She had to figure out what was causing this odd rush of adrenaline.

At last she found a bathrobe, shrugged into it and padded across the hall to peer down into Cody's crib. The baby lay peacefully sleeping. So why did she still feel this sense of impending disaster? As she slipped her feet into her bedroom slippers, a shrill ringing split the silence. The doorbell this early?

The emergency had come to her doorstep! She took the steps two at a time, flicked on the light in the foyer and unlocked the door, bracing herself for whatever awaited her.

Her parents stood in the predawn darkness.

"Mom, Dad!" she exclaimed.

They peered at her with worried eyes, their mouths straight and grim as she ushered them inside. Her mother's auburn hair hadn't been curled, and her lips hadn't been polished their usual frosted pink. "Are you okay, honey?" she asked Elissa with perplexing concern.

"Me? Of course I'm okay. What's this all about?"

Her parents exchanged an anxious glance, and her lanky, silver-haired father said, "Dean stopped by."

She stared at them in dismay. He must have gone straight from here to their house. What had he told them? She turned away from their probing eyes and led them out of the foyer. "What did he tell you?"

Her mother watched her anxiously. "He said you think you're being...haunted."

Her lips tightened with anger at Dean. She hadn't expected such a low blow. "Dean and I had a disagreement, and I asked him to leave. But other than that, everything's perfectly—" Her assurance broke off as she flicked on a wall switch that illuminated the living room.

The place resembled a war zone. Shattered glass glinted in the debris that littered the Persian carpet and flagstone floor—books, vases, paintings, model ships, sculptures, rose petals, popcorn. Every lamp in the room had been smashed; every picture yanked off its moorings. Her parents gaped at the wreckage in stunned silence. She searched her mind for an explanation, but couldn't think of one.

At a little shriek from her mother, Elissa swung around to see her pointing at the gold letter opener buried a good inch in the wall where Jesse had barely missed Dean's head last night. "Dean told us about that," whispered her mother, aghast. "Oh, Elissa, you could have killed him!"

"I didn't throw that at Dean!"

"Then, who did?" countered her father.

She took refuge in righteous indignation. "I appreciate your concern, but I'm perfectly capable of dealing with my own problems. Dean and I are having difficulties—in fact, we parted ways—but he shouldn't have come to you."

"Your difficulties become my business when they involve your mental health," exploded her father, "and the safety of my grandson." The mention of Cody's safety filled Elissa with new foreboding. Her father continued, "When I get a visit in the middle of the night from a young man who looks like he's been mugged, and he tells me my daughter flew into a rage and attacked him because she thinks she's possessed by the ghost of that no-account drifter who—"

"Don't call Jesse that," she admonished him sharply. "He's the father of my child and deserves your respect."

Her father stared at her incredulously. "Was Dean right, then? You think you're possessed by his…his ghost?"

"Of course not." Her throat closed, and she worked furiously to open it. She wished she could simply tell them the truth, but that would be tantamount to locking herself away in a padded cell. "I do feel a connection with Jesse," she admitted, "emotional more than spiritual. I mentioned that to Dean, and he obviously took it too literally."

"Is that Jesse's robe you're wearing?" asked her father.

She glanced down at the oversized robe and felt her embarrassment rise. "I didn't have time to find my own."

"Staying in his house, wearing his clothes…" Her father looked white, drawn and older than when he'd walked in. "I had no idea," he murmured more to himself than to her.

Anxiety curled like sharp talons in her stomach. "I'm okay, Dad. I swear."

"Of course you are. You're a bright, fine girl." His eyes welled up with sudden shininess. "This Jesse just got under your skin, that's all. You weren't used to men like him. You were too sheltered. You should have dated more."

"I'm going to call the doctor," said her mother in a voice that warbled with unshed tears. "We'll take her to Peachtree Hospital, Walter." She addressed her husband as if Elissa weren't present. "It's one of the best private hospitals in Georgia. She'll get good help there...."

"I'm not going to a hospital, Mom." She couldn't possibly waste that much time when this bewildering sense of urgency beat through her with an even greater force than before. *Hurry. Hurry.* But what crisis called out to her?

"It's for your own good, Elissa," insisted her father. "And for Cody's. We'll take care of him until you're home."

"You'd rather believe I'm crazy than doubt Dean's word?" She tried to forget that she herself had believed him implicitly until Jesse had shown her better.

"Not crazy!" reproved her mother, visibly appalled. "Just...emotionally overwrought. Professional help might ease you through the worst of it, honey. And there's no need to blame Dean. He only confirmed our fears. You haven't been yourself since you met Jesse. Going to bed with him when you didn't even know him. Swearing he was with you after he'd died. Leaving your home and business on an impulse. And now,

look!" Her mother lifted her hands in a gesture that encompassed the ravaged living room. Pain glazed her
eyes as they met Elissa's. "Can't you see that we have to
get some help for you? We can't take the chance of you
hurting yourself, honey. Or hurting others."

Elissa's anger gradually seeped out of her, like air
from a deflating balloon. They were doing what they
truly felt was best for Cody and her. Realizing she'd get
nowhere arguing, she swallowed her pride. "Okay. I'll
see a doctor."

"At Peachtree Hospital," her father pressed. "Today."

AT LEAST HER PARENTS allowed her to take a shower before she left. Most of her luggage would be loaded into
their car by now. Cody, whom she had woken and fed,
would be freshly diapered and dressed.

"Emotionally overwrought," they'd called her. She
couldn't argue with that. She wasn't even sure she
could argue if they'd called her "crazy." If she hadn't
gone at least a little nuts, why was every beat of her
heart reverberating with warnings of disaster?

She leaned her forehead against the glass door of the
shower stall and let the water beat against her. *Jesse, oh,
Jesse, I need you.* But she couldn't allow herself to think
that. What if her own panic somehow drew him back
again from his ultimate destiny?

*Have you found your way to the other side, Jesse? Are you
happy and safe now?* The only answer she received was
an increase in the panic she barely held at bay.

*Believe in me, Elissa,* he had begged her last night. He
had wanted her to believe he wasn't dead, that they
could have a future together. But she'd have to discount

the evidence of her own eyes, her own senses, to believe him.

Her heart whispered, *You were wrong before*.

She had to acknowledge the truth of that. She had come to believe Jesse before only because of cold, hard proof—the business card on which he'd written his address for Dean. Would she ever have believed him— that he hadn't received his mail in time and hadn't deliberately ignored her pregnancy—if she hadn't seen that black-and-white evidence?

She blanched at the mistake she'd almost made in trusting Dean...and remembered the lesson it had taught her: *Listen to your heart*.

But her heart wanted her to believe that Jesse wasn't dead. Which was, of course, preposterous. Wasn't it? An odd, shivery heat crept beneath her skin. At one time, she had considered the existence of ghosts to be preposterous.

As she lathered shampoo into her hair, she thought back to every occurrence, every conversation she'd had with Jesse. She'd reached the conclusion early on that he was a ghost, and assumed he had to be dead. But what if she'd been wrong?

Again the compelling sense of urgency pulsated through her, stronger now than ever. And she saw her own words and actions of the past few days in an entirely different light.

*Oh, God*, she thought with a plummeting heart, *what if I was wrong?*

FULLY DRESSED AND PACKED, she flipped through the cards in her wallet to be sure she had the ones she would need: credit cards, identification, passport. With an anxious glance at the locked bedroom door, she then dialed the number of a travel agency on her cellular phone. Little had Dean known that his gift would provide her with a separate line to the outside world when she needed it most.

"Let's go, Elissa," called her father from outside the bedroom door. "We have a long drive. Dr. Harrison will be waiting for us at the hospital."

"I'm almost ready, Dad."

His footsteps thudded down the stairs. A travel agent answered the phone. In a hushed voice, Elissa inquired about flights to the army base in Asia where Jesse had been stationed. It would take two connecting flights, she was told, and a bus trip to the base. By the time she had mapped out her route, another knock pounded at her door.

"Are you talking to someone?" called her mother. Elissa, however, was in the middle of reading her credit card number to secure a flight. Hushed panic entered her mother's voice. "Walter, I think she's talking to herself in there. Does she think she's with that ghost?"

Breaking her connection, Elissa hurried to open the door. "Calm down, Mom. I'm on the phone."

Her mother gazed at her with both sheepishness and relief. Slipping the cellular phone into her purse, Elissa kissed her mother's pale cheek, scooped up her overnight bag and descended the stairs. "Are you sure you don't mind taking care of Cody?"

Two steps behind her, her mother replied, "Of course we don't mind. We love keeping Cody."

"We'll bring him to visit you," promised her father. She kissed his cheek as she passed him in the foyer. "I'm sure you won't be away from home long," he said reassuringly.

She forced a weak smile, palmed the car keys she had

slipped into her pocket and strode directly out of the door. As she passed her parents' car, she saw Cody in his car seat. She longed to kiss him goodbye, but knew she couldn't risk it. Her parents were convinced she needed to be saved from herself, and they'd stop at nothing to protect her. Tough love, she'd heard it called—although this time, their toughness was somewhat misguided.

Hadn't she practiced "tough love" on Jesse, sending him away for his own good? Had she been similarly misguided?

"Wait a minute, honey, we're taking my car," her father called from the porch as she headed for her own vehicle.

"We'd only have to come back for mine," she said as she slipped in behind the wheel.

Her father hurried to the driver's window, which she obligingly rolled down. "I'd prefer that you ride with me, Elissa. It's not safe for you to drive right now."

She started up the engine. "I'm fine, Dad. And there's something I have to do before I go to the hospital."

"Elissa!" He gripped the window's edge and walked along as she slowly pulled forward.

Her parents' car blocked her from behind; she'd have to drive onto the grass to reach the road....

"Stop this car right now," her father shouted.

"I'm sorry, but I can't." She caught his gaze and held it. "Trust me, Dad. Please. You always have before. Don't stop when I need your faith the most." Swallowing a tightness in her throat, she cut the wheel and drove onto the grass. Her father let go of the window's edge and stared at her. "I'll call you," she promised.

"Elissa!" cried her mother from the porch, "if you

don't come with us right now, we'll...we'll start court proceedings. We'll take custody of Cody!"

She slowed her car as she turned onto the paved road. They'd take Cody from her? It was a mother's fear talking...fear for her daughter, for her grandson. Would she actually carry out the threat? If her parents were truly convinced that she posed a danger, she knew they would.

How could she risk losing her baby? She'd already lost her reputation, her career as a counselor, and Jesse, the love of her life. Now she stood to lose Cody, too.

But how could she not follow up on every lead that might take her to Jesse? She wasn't sure how, where or *if* she'd find him, but this compelling urgency pushed her to look for him—she now felt sure of that much.

If by some miracle she found him, her parents would have to acknowledge that she was acting on more than an insane impulse. Once they realized she wasn't crazy, they'd happily return Cody to her.

But what if she was wrong? What if this sudden need to investigate Jesse's death was nothing more than desperately wishful thinking? Her parents then would have even more grounds to believe she'd lost her mind. "She flew to Asia to look for a dead soldier," they'd tell the psychiatrists. By that time, they'd have found corroborating testimony from others. Like Suzanne, Jesse's housekeeper, who could say, "She thought she was talking to Jesse, but I didn't see anyone." And Dean, who would launch into his lie about how she'd attacked him with the letter opener....

She brought her car to a halt a few yards down the road. Should she go? Should she stay? Her soul cried out for guidance.

*Believe in me, Elissa,* Jesse had begged. *Believe in me.*

Uttering a silent prayer for forgiveness in the event that she was wrong, Elissa clenched her jaw, shifted into gear and pressed the gas pedal steadily to the floor.

# 13

*HE WASN'T GOING TO HELP her.* She'd come all this way—twenty hours in the air, a mad dash to make connections, exhausted sleep in cramped seats and an endless bus ride with chattering locals and their livestock—only to have Colonel Atkinson stare at her from beneath his woolly, copper-colored brows and mutter, "No sense wasting your time and ours, Ms. Sinclair. Captain Garrett is dead."

Elissa leaned forward in a chair beside the colonel's desk. "All I'm asking is to see where the plane went down."

He frowned, his gaze direct, impersonal and alive with an intelligence that had undoubtedly earned him his rank. He was a bear of a man—broad and commanding—and his gruff voice sounded like a growl. "It's a jungle out there. Dangerous. Just what do you hope to find?"

"I'm not sure. I—" She shut her eyes briefly, gathered her courage and countered with a question. "Exactly how much of Jesse's remains were actually found?"

The colonel's lips thinned with impatience. He clearly considered her question a waste of his time. "The plane crashed into a mountainside, Ms. Sinclair. I don't like to be crude, but everyone in that plane was blown to bits. The biggest body part we found was a hip connected to a thigh."

She suspected he was being deliberately shocking. Forcing her into comprehension. She repeated her question with forced composure, "How much of his body was found?"

"I'd have to check with forensics, and even then, I—"

"Please, Colonel. You have to admit that Jesse wasn't like most people. He moved objects with his thoughts and bent metal with his mind. You know he did that, don't you?"

"Well, yes, but—"

"Then, why is it so hard to believe that he contacted me telepathically?"

His frown took on a different quality—a reflective one. "You still think he appeared to you?"

"I *know* he did. He said he heard people talking after the plane crashed. Maybe someone found him and took him in." Something else Jesse had told her surfaced in her memory, but she hesitated to mention it. It may have meant nothing; a figment of delirium. Telling it now might weaken her credibility even more. Then again, Jesse had considered it important enough to relate to her. "There was something else he said, although it didn't make much sense to me."

"What was it?"

"After the plane crash, he heard *you* talking to him."

"Me? Impossible. I was here the entire time."

"He thought you said, 'I'll eat green grits for you.'"

All color drained from the colonel's face. He couldn't have looked more stunned if Jesse himself had appeared. Slowly he turned away and opened his bottom desk drawer.

Elissa's eyes widened as he drew out a gun.

"See this, Ms. Sinclair?" he mumbled, examining the weapon. "This gun won't fire. It's workings are jammed." He glanced up at her. "Jesse was a tough young private when I first heard about his so-called 'powers.' I called him over to me during target practice and told him he was full of bull. He saluted me and said, 'Yes, sir.' I told him to quit the magic shows—this wasn't a kid's party and he wasn't a clown." A brief smile bent the colonel's mouth. "The longer I kept at him, the warmer the gun grew in my hand, until it nearly branded me. I had to drop it." Incredulity glimmered in his eyes even now. "When it cooled enough for me to shoot it, the damned thing was jammed. Permanently."

"Excuse me, Colonel," said Elissa, distracted by the urgency she'd held at bay these last twenty-some hours, "but what does all this have to do with the color of grits?"

He let out a laugh. "Not a damn thing. But it does have to do with the power of Jesse's mind. When I heard about the plane crash, I took out this gun and thought about him. About the good times we'd had, and a bet I'd lost to him over a football game. The payoff was that I'd eat green grits, Savannah-style, every Saint Patrick's Day." His voice grew hoarse. "I said those words out loud after he'd died, Ms. Sinclair. I promised I'd eat green grits for him."

After a solemn moment, he returned the gun to his drawer, picked up the phone and uttered instructions involving forensic files. A while later, he set down the receiver. "There wasn't much of his body found—only one part. But we were able to make a positive identification."

Elissa's heartbeats slowed. "Which part was it?"

"His finger."

"Which finger?"

"Ms. Sinclair, this morbid preoccupation with—"

"Was it his small one? His...pinkie?"

"Why, yes," he replied in surprise. "It was."

She pressed her lips together to stifle a cry. His pinkie finger—the only part of his body in which he'd lost feeling. "Don't you see, Colonel? All that proves is that he lost his finger. The rest of him might still be alive."

"I'd say that's rather a long shot." But he picked up the phone, anyway...to arrange for a vehicle and a driver.

THE SITE OF THE PLANE crash was a whole day's drive from the base. Colonel Atkinson himself accompanied Elissa, along with a driver who spoke the language well enough to translate. They drove on rutted roads canopied by dense, tropical vegetation, questioning ragged farmers and their families who toiled beneath the hot Asian sun, most wearing large straw hats and working in fields, some clustered around thatched-roofed huts. The colonel showed a picture of Jesse he'd taken from his files, and each time, Elissa prayed for a spark of recognition. That spark never came.

Near evening, they checked into a hotel, which necessitated another long drive. The colonel promised they'd continue tomorrow.

Early the next day they set out in determined silence. Elissa's urgency had progressed to full-blown obsession. If not for the colonel's insistence, she would have foregone eating and sleeping. Again, their quest proved fruitless.

"I'm sorry, Ms. Sinclair," he said as they returned to the hotel that second night. "We've covered every village near the crash site. An injured man couldn't have wandered any farther." His voice cracked with disappointment. "I can't justify the time or expense of another day's search."

Exhausted, frustrated, yet driven by a relentless need, Elissa spent half the night pacing in her hotel room. "Jesse," she whispered aloud, "am I wrong to be searching for you? Have you moved on to your everafter?" She waited in the darkness, yearning for a response that didn't come.

But as she fell wearily into bed, she remembered something else he had told her. The people he'd heard talking after the crash had used the word *dakrah*. He'd said it meant "dying." *"It's a word I learned on an undercover mission two years ago, when I worked in an Asian village."*

Could the term be unique to that area—a localism? She hadn't mentioned it to the colonel because it hadn't seemed important. But what if it could pinpoint a region?

She approached the colonel the next morning. He hadn't heard the word *dakrah* before, and neither had his driver. "We have to find out where they use that word," she insisted.

"Ms. Sinclair," the colonel said with a deep weariness, "just because Jesse heard those people talking after the crash doesn't mean that they were physically with him. He heard me, and I was hundreds of miles away. It was probably another psychic thing...."

"He learned that word when he was on an undercover mission in an Asian village two years ago. You'd know where he worked then, wouldn't you?"

"Even if I did, I wouldn't be at liberty to tell you."

"Is it anywhere near the crash site?"

He raised his eyes to the ceiling as if praying for the patience to deal with her. "Do you understand the

meaning of undercover, Ms. Sinclair? Covert? Top secret, maybe?"

"If you won't help me, Colonel, I'll contact the embassy, universities, language experts, investigative re-
porters—*anyone* who could help me pinpoint where the
word *dakrah* is used. Then I'll hire a guide to take me
there."

"You'll get yourself killed," he growled, his neck
turning a dull red, "and compromise security in the
process."

"I'll try my best not to."

He stared hard at her for a long while. "You never
say die, do you."

"I did once," she whispered through a tightened
throat. "I won't make that mistake again."

Later that day, Colonel Atkinson checked Jesse's files
and located the village where he'd worked undercover
two years ago. It lay just beyond where they had
searched.

He then ordered a background check on one Elissa
Sinclair. When it came back clean, he reached a decision
that ran contrary to his usual prudence—mostly because he knew this particular woman would make his
job a living hell if he didn't. He took her to that village.

"This place has been a hotbed of military unrest for
the past decade," he warned as their jeep made its way
down the muddy road of the village with its thatched
huts and sloping farms surrounded by wooded mountain peaks. "Soldiers of any kind won't be welcomed
here."

Not a comforting thought, reflected Elissa, considering they were riding in a military vehicle driven by a
fully armed, uniformed soldier in the presence of his
commanding officer.

"If Jesse isn't here—and I seriously doubt he is," he muttered, "these people won't know that he was a U.S. soldier. He worked here posing as a civilian volunteer. It would be damaging to our cause and dangerous for any current or future deployments to advertise the fact that we planted a spy here. We're not going to flash his picture around. The only one I have shows him in uniform. We're simply going to ask the villagers if they know anything about an injured American. We'll say your husband is missing, and that the embassy sent me to help you look for him. One thing is very important, Elissa. Let me do all the talking."

She nodded, her hope riding high in her throat. The driver stopped to begin his questioning, and she noticed the villagers' reluctance to approach. She heard him use the word *dakrah,* and they nodded in apparent understanding. Then they shook their heads and backed away.

"But he has to be here," she said, her hands balled into tight fists in her lap. "He has to be."

They stopped at each hut along the winding mud road. Villagers trailed them, watching with suspicious eyes. No one, it seemed, had seen or heard about a man found injured.

But as the afternoon grew late and the driver questioned the family at the last home in the village, Elissa gave in to desperation. Shouldering her way past the driver, she begged the ragged farmer, "Please, *please* try to remember if you've heard anything about an injured stranger. He's tall, with dark hair. His little finger is missing." She held up her hand and waggled her pinkie finger.

From the blank gazes of the farmer and his family, she knew her pleading was useless—they probably didn't understand a word—but she couldn't bring herself to stop. "He was hurt in an accident. He might be dying. *Dakrah...*"

"They can't help us," the colonel interrupted, coming up behind her and taking her arm. "Let's go, Elissa."

Stricken, she stared at him as if he'd condemned her to death. In a way, he had. He was taking away all hope....

"Ay-lees-a?" echoed an elderly woman from the family hovering behind the farmer. "You...Ay-lees-a?"

Startled, she replied, "Yes, I'm Elissa."

The woman's mouth opened wider, and her wrinkled hand came up to cover it. She then whispered something fast and fierce to a younger woman. The farmer muttered in angry disapproval, and a muted argument broke out among them.

Elissa exchanged a puzzled glance with the colonel and his driver. Why should her name cause bickering?

The elderly woman finally broke away from the huddle, and despite the farmer's tight-lipped glare, she ventured closer, her graying head held high. There was no mistaking her for anything other than the matriarch of the family. "You stay," she ordered. "GIs go."

The farmer uttered some oath and threw his hands up. The colonel barked, "What? We can't leave her here!"

The driver snorted a contemptuous, "No can do."

Elissa spoke only to the old woman, whose eyes were fixed on hers. "Do you know something about an injured man?"

"No." She shook her head and pointed toward the road that led down the mountain. "GIs go. You stay."

After a bewildered moment, Elissa turned to the colonel. "Please do as she asks."

"I can't leave you here! Who knows why she wants you to stay?" Quietly, he muttered, "Some folks have mighty odd customs. You might end up married to one of her grandsons."

"Or held hostage," warned the driver beneath his breath.

"I'll stay. Or—" she deliberated "—I could always return later, on my own...."

Tight-lipped with disapproval that matched the farmer's, the colonel handed her a radio. "If I don't hear from you within one hour, we'll be back to find you."

"Thank you." A sheen of gratitude blurred her vision.

He shook his head. "Never thought I'd say this to any woman, but you're a damned good match for Jesse." Brushing past the driver, he climbed into the jeep. The soldier reluctantly slid behind the wheel.

The small mob of villagers, who had been watching from a distance, gazed in stony silence at the military vehicle as it drove down the muddy road. The moment the jeep was out of sight, the old woman snatched the radio from Elissa. "Me keep." Tucking it into the folds of her long, loose dress, she hobbled across the grass onto the muddy road.

Swallowing her trepidation, Elissa followed.

The hike down the narrow path that wound through dense, tropical growth was not a long one, but altogether unnerving as she dodged a snake-laden limb, crashed through spiderwebs and listened to the hum, buzz and hiss of unseen wildlife.

When they reached their destination, she gaped in astonishment at a huge, two-story stone house. A spaceship wouldn't have surprised her more in this primitive village.

A convent, she deduced, or maybe a mission. Two slim nuns in white stood talking near the front door, and another worked in the garden. Elissa's elderly guide approached the nuns and spoke in low tones while gesturing toward Elissa.

A stern-faced nun addressed her in halting English. Elissa recognized her accent as French. The nun didn't smile; her look was more distrustful than even the villagers'. "Your name?"

"Elissa Sinclair."

"You come with soldiers, *oui?*"

Remembering the colonel's warning about this region's chronic military upheavals, she firmly asserted, "They're only helping me search for my...my husband."

"Your husband?" She glanced down at Elissa's left hand, which bore no ring. "This husband...he is not a soldier?"

Remembering the colonel's fear of blowing Jesse's cover, Elissa floundered. If Jesse was here, would they know he was a soldier? He would have been wearing a uniform—wouldn't he? Could it have been burnt or torn beyond recognition...?

The nun's thin brows rose. "It seems you do not know. Maybe you can tell me his name?"

Again Elissa stared, nonplussed. Would they know his real name—or the one he'd used when he worked undercover? The colonel hadn't told her the name Jesse'd used; he hadn't wanted her to know it, or to speak to these people at all. He hadn't felt comfortable "compromising security" any more than was strictly necessary.

"I...I call him Jesse," she finally answered.

"We have no 'Jesse' in our hospital," she stated. "No

strangers here at all. You and your soldiers can go away."

Disappointment, awful in its power, racked Elissa with piercing pain. "No, please, wait!" she cried. "You might know him by another name. I'm not sure what, but... He's tall and dark, and he's missing a finger." *She couldn't leave this place without him.* Digging wildly in her purse like the madwoman she'd become, she yanked out her wallet and fumbled through the pictures until she came to one of Cody. "Look, sister, look! Do you see this chin? Jesse has the same chin! Yes, and his eyes—they look very much like these—not the color, but the shape. And his nose...you might recognize that nose...." She looked up from the photo with a soul-deep desperation. Like a victim sinking in quicksand, she glanced at each woman around her, from face to unreadable face in a speechless plea. If he wasn't here...if she couldn't find him...if she never saw him again...

Something in the nun's gaze lost its granite edge. "Come inside, *madame*," she murmured, "out of this heat."

Amazed that her body could respond when her mind and heart whirled in the throes of agony, Elissa allowed herself to be guided into the side entrance of the stone house and through its cool, dim interior. Vaguely, she was aware of other nuns, other people, but she couldn't focus on them.

"One of our patients," said the nun in a conversational tone as she led the way down a corridor that smelled of illness and antiseptic, "is a man who worked in our village. A good man, who helped us save lives."

She stopped outside a door and rested her hand on its knob. "In monsoon rains he went out into jungle alone to find a lost child. He sucked poison from snakebite in an old man's leg. He gave his own blood to save a dying baby. We would never turn him over to soldiers, *madame*. Never." The passion in her voice left no doubt about her devotion. "Our boys found him wandering. I do not know how he managed to walk. He is badly hurt." As she pushed open the door, her gaze bore solemnly into Elissa's. "By the time they brought him to us, he was unconscious. He will not wake." Softly, she added, "But in his sleep, *madame*, he calls your name."

Trancelike, Elissa approached the bed, which was wired with life support tubing and monitors. There lay a man, obviously comatose, his face heavily bearded and scabbed, his body and head swathed in bandages.

*Jesse.*

"You think you have found him," whispered the nun, her voice choked with sorrow. "His body is here, yes. But his soul, I think, is not."

# 14

SHE COULDN'T SPEAK, not even a whisper, so tightly clenched was every muscle in her throat. Nor could she cry; her emotions ran too deep for tears.

But she could touch him—at long last she could touch him—and that realization almost undid her. She lay trembling fingers against the only smooth, uninjured skin on his face—along his protruding cheekbone, just above the gaunt hollow darkened by his overgrown beard. As her fingertips rested there, a fierce love washed through her...and a profound, unearthly awe.

She'd only touched this man once before. A year ago.

These large, dark hands that lay bandaged at his sides had not stirred her to feverish passion in these past couple of weeks. These wide, pale lips had not kissed her into sweet delirium. These eyes, now closed, had not glinted with seductive intent as he'd whispered to her beside his bedroom hearth. These arms had not crushed her against him.

No, all the while she'd been falling deeper in love with him at his brick cottage on Isle of Hope, this man had been lying here, still as death, thousands of miles away.

"Oh, God, Jesse," she whispered through an aching throat, "you reached out to me and I...I..." The ache grew too sharp to continue. She had done much worse than merely turn him away—she'd deliberately urged him on toward death.

Her tears began then—bitter, recriminating tears—and sobs that violently shook her. She lay her face against his chest and cried with every ounce of energy left in her—cried for the mistakes she had made, for the time she had wasted, for the love she had withheld.

She had told him she didn't love him.

"I'm so sorry, Jesse. If only I'd believed you."

"Don't cry," soothed the nun, stroking her hair. "You cannot blame yourself. There was nothing you could have done. We tried everything."

But in her heart, she believed she could have made a difference...or else why would he have reached out for her in such a powerful, compelling way? She had wanted to know his goal, his unresolved business. He had tried to tell her—it was life itself.

"Come, have some tea," urged the nun, "and maybe something to eat. You are much too pale."

Elissa wouldn't go; wouldn't move from his side, not for a minute. What was it the colonel had said to her? *You never say die, do you.* Lifting her head, she gazed at Jesse's deathly pale face and swore not to say it now. There had to be a way to bring him back. She would move heaven and earth, if need be. "I have to call the colonel," she said. "He'll bring doctors, medicine, equipment...."

"No, no, you must not tell the soldiers!" cried the nun.

Elissa frowned, uncomprehending.

"When our boys found him, he was wearing a soldier's uniform, or what was left of it. We do not know why. If he is American soldier, there are those here who would kill him. If he is not, the American army might kill him as spy!" The nun shook her head. "You must not tell the soldiers he is here. It could mean death for him—and much trouble for us."

Elissa covered the nun's hand with her own. "There will be no trouble from the soldiers, I promise. Colonel Atkinson is a good man. We can trust him."

"But it will do no good, asking for more doctors and medicine. The doctor who works here with us studied at your American universities. He said we cannot move him. His condition has worsened in these last few days. We called a priest to his side, *madame*. Your husband...he is dying."

"Find the woman who has the radio," instructed Elissa. "If I don't call the colonel or he doesn't find me, there will be much more trouble for this village... believe me."

With a sharp intake of breath, the nun paled, nodded and hurried off to find the radio.

HE WAS NO LONGER speeding through the long, dark tunnel. He now drifted weightlessly, barely moving at all. He'd lost all sense of time, or maybe time had simply lost its meaning. The drifting calmed him, lulled him. Lessened the pain...

The darkness began to flicker into colors, shapes, sounds. Like a three-dimensional movie, forms took shape. His mother, his aunt, his family. Scenes played out. His life, he realized, every moment, thought and emotion. Hurtful ones, mostly, in his early life. Loneliness, anger, shame.

As he grew, his defenses toughened, and even those emotions lost strength. He lived life on its surface. Never deep, except when he faced danger and adrenaline pumped him full of emotion. Only then did he truly feel. There was plenty of danger to keep him going, mission after mission.

And then suddenly, there she was—*Elissa*. Like a dam bursting, emotions gushed in fierce, unstoppable currents—warm, deep emotions—flooding every corner of his soul. Elissa. He'd had to leave her for another mission. His last mission. A hellish one made more so because he had tasted a richness he now craved.

The pace of his remembering slowed, and he saw himself boarding the plane for home. The premonition of death had been riding in his gut and now sharpened as he stepped on board. He read Elissa's letters, longed to see her and the son they'd made. Then the pilot's voice came over the intercom, talking about engine trouble. The plane rolled, angled into a dive. Panic broke out among the men.

But then the aircraft leveled out. The pilot announced that the problem had been fixed. "Relax, boys. You're on your way home." The men cheered and joked with giddy relief.

Jesse knew better. They had to leave the plane or they'd die. He strode down the aisle to the cockpit and informed the pilot of the danger. He couldn't pinpoint the problem, though; he couldn't explain. The pilot muttered bland assurances and strained to see through thickening fog.

Jesse went back to the men, his sense of impending disaster throbbing. "Prepare to jump."

They stared at him in disbelief.

"But we're going home, sir."

"The danger's over."

"No need to jump now, sir."

He reworded his terse command into a direct order. As the men exchanged stunned glances, he prepared his own gear and moved to the emergency exit.

"B-but that might be hostile territory below, sir," stammered a young soldier.

"We'll head north," he told him. "I have contacts...."

"But we're headed home, sir," said another.

They weren't responding to his order.

"You always said you wouldn't expect us to do anything you wouldn't do, sir."

"Yeah—you go first."

He felt the danger nearing. Angry, determined, he opened the hatch and shouted for them to obey. The plane took another roll, lurching him forward. He felt himself falling, falling. He yanked his cord, his chute burst open, and he was jerked upward by the billowing canvas. An explosion thundered above him. Pain struck like a poisonous spear. His hand...his hand had been hit by the debris.... And then a pain jolted through his head. Images jumbled. He tried hard to hold on to the survival skills that had kept him alive for the last fifteen years—he had to shrug free of his gear, trek to familiar ground—but darkness pressed in on him. Darkness that grew ever deeper...

"Jesse!"

Was that Elissa's voice? It spiraled through him with a glowing, visceral warmth. But it couldn't be her. She hadn't wanted him. Hadn't loved him enough. She'd sent him toward his death....

The colors and shapes faded into a dim, solitary point. Gradually, though, it brightened and grew...this time into a brilliant white beacon. Irresistibly, it drew him.

COLONEL ATKINSON SPENT the evening with Elissa by Jesse's bedside, uttering profuse apologies for not having believed her sooner, praising her courage for sticking by her convictions. "You did it, Elissa. You found him, and now I'll make damn sure he gets the best care that money and rank can buy. We've got the finest specialists in the world standing by. We'll airlift him out of here in the morning."

Elissa nearly cried with gratitude. The colonel believed there was hope...virtually *promised* that Jesse would pull through. For the first time since she'd found him, sweet hope buoyed her up. She fell asleep in a chair beside his bed, holding tightly on to that optimism.

A shrill ringing startled her awake—an alarm on some monitor—and a young nun shouted into the intercom in rapidfire French.

"What is it?" cried Elissa, stumbling half dazed from the chair. "What's happened?" It didn't take medical training to soon understand—the monitor at Jesse's bedside had ceased graphing its rhythmic peaks and valleys...and now hummed, showing a steady, flat line. His heart had ceased to beat.

Elissa stared in numb, horrified disbelief. How could this be? The colonel was going to airlift him out of here this morning...he'd get the very best of help....

The room burst into activity—nuns, nurses and doctors swarmed around, yelling instructions to one another, pushing her aside as they clustered around Jesse. In a haze of shock, she realized they were administering emergency treatment, trying to jolt his heart into action. She heard counting, buzzing, banging and occasional muffled sobs.

Then all of it stopped...and there was only weeping.

All but one doctor had backed away from the bed, Elissa realized. "It's no good," someone whispered, "he's gone."

*Gone.*

She somehow found her way to Jesse's side. Everyone, everything, faded from view but the man lying so still before her. "Don't do this, Jesse." The voice she heard was her own—quiet, but steady. "Come away from that light. Come away from it, do you hear? I was wrong to send you toward it. It's not time for you to die. Come back to me!"

Hands clutched at her, tried to pull her away. She shrugged them off, reached for Jesse's face, held it between her palms. "We could have a life together. A good life. You and Cody and I. You can raise him, be his father. He needs you. Cody needs you, Jesse!"

She gazed down hard at him, willing him to respond. Her desperation turned into anger. "You told me you'd defy death itself for a lifetime of loving me. If you meant it, Jesse, do it now," she ordered, her teeth clenching. "Do it!"

"*Madame*, he cannot," murmured a sad voice from behind her. "You must let him go."

"Did you lie to me, then, Jesse?" she cried, ignoring the nun's somber words. "Did you lie to me, damn you?" In her mind's eye, she saw him frowning. But not the slightest movement disturbed his face.

As suddenly as it came, her anger left her. She swept her hand into his hair, and her voice broke. "No, you didn't lie. You never have. You never would." Anguish welled up to choke her. "Please, Jesse, please," she said, sobbing. "Come back to me. I need you. I love you. I love you!"

Although the liquid heat in her eyes blinded her, she saw him quite clearly with her heart. As the distant hum of a monitor broke up into slow but distinct beeps, a harsh wheezing sound erupted from the bed. *An indrawn breath.*

And Jesse opened his eyes.

# Epilogue

IT HAD BEEN A DAY of surprises. A month of them, actually, Jesse reflected, as he lathered soap across his chest and let the steamy, pulsating shower beat against his deeply scarred back and shoulders.

He still hadn't gotten over the shock of waking in that hospital to find Elissa at his side, swearing that she loved him. Some things are just too good to take in all at once; he planned to savor *that* surprise for a long while to come.

When he had realized the lengths she'd gone to and the danger she'd faced—grateful though he was that she found him—he damn near kicked the colonel's butt for letting her. The only thing that stopped him, other than his deep respect for the man and his rank, was the fact that he knew how hell-bent stubborn the woman could be. The colonel might make his Special Force commandos quake in their boots, but he hadn't really stood a chance against Elissa Sinclair.

Or rather, Elissa Sinclair Garrett. A fission of warmth, pride and something too profound to define spiraled through Jesse. She was his now.

He'd married her before they'd even left the hospital, though the marriage so far had been in name only. It had taken weeks of full-time therapy in the finest Georgia hospital to get back the full, fluent use of his body. His mental faculties, however, according to the astonished doctors, remained as sharp as if he hadn't lost consciousness at all during his month-long coma.

Jesse smiled. As far as comas went, his had been a relatively pleasant one. Damned pleasant.

And if the doctors wondered at his quick recuperation, it was only because they hadn't gazed into Elissa's eyes to see what awaited him there. They hadn't suffered the temptation of her kisses...the sweet, intoxicating ones that made him push himself harder than his therapists recommended. He ached for more than her gazes, for more than her soul-stirring kisses. He wanted to possess her, his wife, entirely.

He would do so tonight.

They'd be alone—without nurses, therapists, doctors or well-meaning friends—for the first time since he'd woken from the coma. He'd made sure of that by booking a suite in an out-of-the-way Savannah hotel where no one would find them.

Not an easy task when the colonel had invited soldiers from all corners of the globe to surprise him with a reception today. Men he hadn't seen in years showed up, embarrassing him with stories of how he'd saved their lives or rescued them from danger. As if they hadn't all done their part at some time or another to keep *his* butt alive.

But Elissa had taken in all their nonsense, glowing up at him as if he were some hero.

Her parents had been there, too, listening to the tributes. Her mother, with eyes very much like Elissa's, cried and hugged him. Her father made a toast, welcomed him to his family and called him his son. Warm, unfamiliar sensations had crowded Jesse's chest.

His own mother had been at the reception, although he doubted she heard the speeches. She'd been silently daydreaming in the chair beside him. At one point, though, she had noticed his dress uniform with all its ribbons and medals—the uniform Colonel Atkinson insisted he wear—and whispered, "You look like your father. He had a uniform, too. Air force, I think." Sadly, she added, "He was killed in the war, you know."

Jesse had stared at her, astonished. She'd never spoken about his father before. Even more surprising was the fond, reminiscent look on her face. "You kept in touch with him?" he asked, disbelieving.

"He wrote me letters. Asked for pictures of you."

A sneak attack by a stealth bomber wouldn't have surprised him more. "But I thought... Hadn't he... hadn't he hurt you?" Another first—Jesse had never asked her about the rape his aunt had so often mentioned.

His mother's forehead wrinkled and her eyes glazed with confusion, as if she weren't quite sure what he meant.

Gently, he persisted, "Didn't he force you to...to *do* something you hadn't wanted to do?"

"Oh, no." Her childlike blue eyes widened. "Robert would never make me do anything I didn't want. He was always nice to me."

Jesse frowned. "He didn't rape you?"

She blinked, still looking confused. "Muriel said he did. She said Robert should have known better, even if I didn't tell him no. She wouldn't lie to me...would she?"

It had, indeed, been a surprising day. Looking back, Jesse reflected that his Aunt Muriel had been wise to stay away from the reception. She wouldn't want to hear the things he had to say to her.

His cousin Dean had also been noticeably absent. Not that this surprised or bothered Jesse in the least. He hoped his boot was still imprinted on his pompous backside.

Jesse's mother had shared one more bit of news: because she was going to marry and live with that nice preacher who spoke at his funeral—a lovely funeral; Jesse should have seen it—her sister Muriel planned to sell her town house in Savannah and move in with her son. To help get Dean's life in order, Muriel had told her...

Jesse couldn't help a satisfied grin as he turned off the shower. Muriel and Dean deserved each other.

As he pushed aside the vinyl shower curtain, he heard it—soft murmurs issuing from the bedroom. Disappointment drew his mouth down into a frown. Was someone here? Whoever it was, he'd throw them out. Shove 'em right out the door. This was *his* night with Elissa, the start of their honeymoon, and he meant to monopolize every second of it.

A year, two months, and too many weeks had gone by since this body of his had taken hers. He needed that now. Needed the passionate insanity that somehow made his spirit soar. Needed to know that after all he'd been through, he could still make her tremble in his arms and cry out his name....

It was Elissa's voice he heard, he realized as he slung a towel around his hips. Soft, loving sounds. Who the *hell* was she talking to? Bewildered, he pushed open the bathroom door, his hair dripping in little rivulets down his neck and shoulders.

She lounged against a mound of pillows, her long, sable dark hair flowing loosely around her slender form, with some black, wispy little lace thing doing nothing at all to hide the feminine curves and valleys that so intrigued him. Where the black lace ended, her golden legs stretched for miles along the bedspread, from

thighs to shapely calves, crossed with seductive allure....

A telephone receiver, he belatedly noticed, was
pressed against her ear. "I love you, baby," she murmured in a low, fervent voice into the mouthpiece. "I
miss you. Do you miss me? Don't worry, we'll be together soon...."

Every muscle in Jesse's body froze. For an instant—
the briefest, blackest instant—the euphoria of the day
evaporated, and he was once again the outsider, battle-
scarred and deformed, pressing his nose against the
window and peering in at a warmth he'd never know....

But before his heart had even missed a beat, a new,
awesome certainty embraced him. *He could believe in her.*
If he trusted his heart to pump his blood, if he trusted
his lungs to draw in breath, he could trust this woman
to love him; she'd been far more constant than either.
When his body itself had failed him, she had not. She
never would.

As though sensing his presence, Elissa lifted her gaze.
She smiled a warm, dazzling smile that blazed a path of
love straight through his heart. "Know who else is
here?" she murmured into the phone. "Your old pa."

And she handed the receiver to Jesse.

He took it by rote, overcome by awe that he, of all
men, had been blessed with her. And though he had no
idea why she'd be talking over the phone to Cody—he
wouldn't understand her; couldn't even *talk* yet, let
alone answer questions—Jesse dutifully lifted the receiver to his ear.

"Hey, there, boy," he heard himself say, his voice too
deep and rusty. Before he knew it, he found himself listening closely for the slightest gurgle. Clearly he imagined a phone being held against that little rounded
cheek; saw his son's bright gaze, maybe teary-eyed

from wanting his mother. "Love you, Cody," he muttered hoarsely. "We'll be home soon, just wait and see."

As he murmured the kind of nonsense he never imagined would come from his mouth, a torrent of goodness, warmth and light flooded him. He was whole. He was healed.

He was loved.

A slender hand swept up his leg and tugged at his towel. "Tell him good night" came the throaty feminine voice that set a thousand flames licking through his veins.

"'Night, son," he breathed. The receiver had barely hit its cradle before he'd tossed aside the towel and lowered himself to the bed.

"I love you, Jesse," Elissa swore in a solemn whisper.

His hands delved beneath the black lace and swept along bare, silken flesh. His arms filled with fragrant, womanly warmth; his mouth connected hungrily with hers. He loved her so much it hurt. She was his, all his, and they'd spend the rest of their lives doing just this— proving, probing, exploring their love for each other.

*Till death do us part*, she had promised.

But for Jesse, that wasn't good enough.

He wanted longer.

Spoil yourself next month
with these four novels from

## CHRISTMAS MALE by Heather MacAllister

*Mail Order Men*

Rusty Romero was flabbergasted! Her grandmother had *actually*
answered a personal ad for her. But Rusty could see why—Trent
Creighton *was* drop-dead gorgeous. Trouble was, his ideas about
women were from the Stone Age! He needed a lesson in
women's lib—and Rusty was just the woman to give him one!

## CHRISTMAS KNIGHT by Lyn Ellis

*Rebels and Rogues*

The only thing Tara Amberly wanted for Christmas was Nick
DeSalvo—to make him pay for his part in her brother's death.
But dealing with an irresistible ex-cop wasn't easy—especially
when the real culprits came on the scene. Suddenly, she found
herself on the run with Nick...and the last thing on her mind was
getting even...

## CHRISTMAS WITH EVE by Elda Minger

*It Happened One Night*

'Twas the night before Christmas...and Eve Vaughn was sharing
the most passionate night of her life with a sexy stranger. She
was determined she'd sneak away the next morning, never to see
him again. But, to Max, she'd been a very special gift—and he
had no intention of letting her go on Christmas Morn...

## TEMPTING JAKE by Molly Liholm

Jake Collins was six foot two inches of raw male animal with
bedroom eyes and a gorgeous smile. Not the kind of man Nora
Stevens expected to be the driver of a holiday coach! He watched
everybody, and was bent on seducing her... The man was *trouble*.

# MILLS & BOON®

---

## Season's Greetings
## To all our readers!

---

The Season's Greetings Gift Pack brings you four
fabulous romances from star-studded authors
including Betty Neels.

And as an extra special Christmas treat we're
offering the pack at a discounted price of just
£6.60––that's 4 books for the price of 3.

*The Mistletoe Kiss* by Betty Neels
*Merry Christmas* by Emma Darcy
*The Faithful Wife* by Diana Hamilton
*Home for Christmas* by Ellen James

Available: November 1997

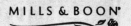

MILLS & BOON®

# Christmas Treats

## A sparkling new anthology
## —the perfect Christmas gift!

Celebrate the season with a taste of love in this
delightful collection of brand-new short stories
combining the pleasures of food and love.

**Figgy Pudding**
by PENNY JORDAN
**All the Trimmings**
by LINDSAY ARMSTRONG
**A Man For All Seasonings**
by DAY LECLAIRE

And, as an extra treat, we've included the
authors' own recipe ideas in this
collection—because no yuletide would be
complete without...Christmas Dinner!

# FREE!

## FOUR FREE
## specially selected
## Temptation® novels
## <u>PLUS</u> a FREE Mystery Gift
## when you return this page...

Return this coupon and we'll send you 4 romances from the Temptation series and a mystery gift absolutely FREE! We'll even pay the postage and packing for you.

We're making you this offer to introduce you to the benefits of the Reader Service™– FREE home delivery of brand-new Temptation novels, at least a month before they are available in the shops, FREE gifts and a monthly Newsletter packed with information, competitions, author profiles and lots more...

Accepting these FREE books and gift places you under no obligation to buy, you may cancel at any time, even after receiving just your free shipment. Simply complete the coupon below and send it to:

MILLS & BOON READER SERVICE, FREEPOST, CROYDON, SURREY, CR9 3WZ.

READERS IN EIRE PLEASE SEND COUPON TO PO BOX 4546, DUBLIN 24

## NO STAMP NEEDED

Yes, please send me 4 free Temptation novels and a mystery gift. I understand that unless you hear from me, I will receive 4 superb new titles every month for just £2.20* each, postage and packing free. I am under no obligation to purchase any books and I may cancel or suspend my subscription at any time, but the free books and gift will be mine to keep in any case. (I am over 18 years of age)

T7YE

Ms/Mrs/Miss/Mr_____
BLOCK CAPS PLEASE

Address_____

_____

_____ Postcode _____

# GET TO KNOW
# THE BEST OF ENEMIES

## the latest blockbuster from TAYLOR SMITH

**_Who would you trust with your life? Think again._**

_Linked to a terrorist bombing, a young student goes
missing. One woman believes in the girl's innocence
and is determined to find her before she is silenced.
Leya Nash has to decide—quickly—who to trust.
The wrong choice could be fatal._

Valid only in the UK & Ireland against purchases made in retail outlets
and not in conjunction with any Reader Service or other offer.

# 50p OFF
## COUPON
**VALID UNTIL: 28.2.1998**

### TAYLOR SMITH'S _THE BEST OF ENEMIES_

9 904170 200509 >

0472 00189